C000072206

CLOCKWISE

A YOUNG ADULT TIME TRAVEL ROMANCE

LEE STRAUSS

la
plume
PRESS

THE CLOCKWISE COLLECTION

Clockwise
Clockwiser
Like Clockwork
Counter Clockwise
Clockwork Crazy
Clocked

COPYRIGHT

CLOCKWISE

by Lee Strauss

(previously published under the names Elle Strauss and Elle Lee Strauss)

Copyright © 2011 Lee Strauss

Cover by Steven Novak Illustrations

ISBN: 9781988677262

This is a work of fiction and the views expressed herein are the sole responsibility of the author. Likewise, characters, places and incidents are either the product of the author's imagination or are represented fictitiously and any resemblance to actual persons, living or dead, or actual event or locales, is entirely coincidental.

All rights reserved.

This book, or parts thereof, may not be reproduced in any form without permission.

*to my wonderful daughter Tasia Strauss
there are a million reasons why*

ONE

EVERYONE HAS TO LIVE with something.

For instance, my hair is the unmanageable kind of curly, the color of burnt toast. Imagine waking up every morning looking like the Lion King, or having to spend a disproportionate amount of your allowance on hair products that don't deliver. Like the ones under my bathroom sink. Row after row of half-empty containers of mousse, gel, and hair tamer standing dejectedly like the third string of a basketball team that rarely gets to play.

The thing is, I would be fine with rag mop hair, truly, if only I didn't have this other issue: uncontrolled time travel to the nineteenth century. I've never met anyone else with the same problem, either, so that also classifies me as some kind of freak.

On the upside—like a blind girl who ultra develops her other senses to compensate for what she can't control—I've picked up a few extra skills along the way. One survival reflex I've nurtured is how to be quick on my feet. I have good impulses, you could say.

Well, normally, this is an upside.

Until a second ago.

I was sitting with my best friend, Lucinda, on the sidelines of the football field. As usual, we were watching the yummy football players, rather than the scrimmage going on because really, who cared about the actual game? Despite the glare of the setting sun, I saw the brown speck hurtling towards me.

Impulsively, I jumped up and thump, Nate Mackenzie's football, signed by the famed Tom Brady himself, was in my arms. I couldn't believe it. I'd caught Nate Mackenzie's ball!

Gingerly, I raised my head. Sauntering across the field, with all his hunky hotness, was the cutest boy in the school, the most valuable senior varsity football player of Cambridge High, and the love of my life. He stopped right in front of me.

"Good catch." His rugged and manly voice lassoed me. He'd said *good catch*. I couldn't move or take my eyes off his face. The way the sun glistened off his sweat, emphasizing his strong jaw and the brightness of his blue eyes, brighter still because of the contrast of his dark, shaggy hair...

"So, can I have my ball back?"

My hands gripped his football with sticky sweat. The ticker tape in my brain searched for the right response before flashing ERROR in red neon twelve-point font.

"Casey?" Lucinda nudged my back. With a slight swivel of my head I saw her expression. Mortification. *Give the dumb ball back!* Did I just have an aneurysm? I felt woozy, like throwing up. I imagined myself vomiting all over Nate's feet.

Unbelievably, there are some things worse than puking in front of the football team. A wave of dizziness threatened to wash me away into black nothingness. But I couldn't be so lucky to just faint. It was happening. Oh no. Not here. *Please, not in front of Nate Mackenzie.*

In an instant, my world brightened like a nuclear blast as I spiraled through a long white tunnel. When I opened my eyes, he was gone. Nate was gone and so were Lucinda and all of Nate's football team.

I stood alone, in the middle of a lush forest painted every shade of green. My lungs filled with the sweet scent of undamaged air, my skin tingled with warm humidity. The furry and feathered inhabitants squealed and chirped with enthusiasm. I heard an unwelcome whistling noise and a pop. Nate's ball, still in my hands, had an arrow sticking out of it.

So much for quick thinking and quick feet. I jumped behind a tree and hid as a couple of kids, maybe ten and twelve, cantered by on horseback.

"You missed it!" teased the older boy. The fortunate squirrel scurried up the tree, its little feet loosening bits of bark that rained down on my head. I could have been killed or at least drastically injured, but all I could think about was Nate's football. The air seeped out as I tugged on the hand-whittled arrow. I slid down the side of the tree and groaned.

Tom Brady's signature had a puncture hole right in the middle of it. I gripped the flattened ball as I stomped through the brush, pushing scratchy branches away from my face. *Why did this have to happen in front of Nate Mackenzie? Why?*

Pack your bags, self-pity. I was cursed with time traveling. I was a slave to it with no control over when or *in front of who* it happens, and as far as I knew there was no cure. Not that I had anyone to ask about it. I just had to survive, which fortunately, I'd gotten pretty good at.

I soon came to a wide dirt road scarred with uneven grooves ground in by irregular carriage travel and dotted with hazardous looking empty potholes. I imagined they filled up unattractively with muddy water when it rained. A waist-high rectangular stone marker, leaning slightly like a wounded soldier, had the miles to Cambridge MA etched in it. Good. I knew where I was.

Time travel, as expected, is fraught with complications. The immediate one is what to wear. Or more like what not to wear. As in blue jeans and sneakers I needed to ditch ASAP. I slipped back into the dense covering of the forest and kept hiking. The second immediate problem has to do with food and drink. Let's just say that to solve these problems, you have to get creative.

I recognized a thick grove of lilac bushes and pushed my way through to the center, where a patch of wild grass opened up like a bald spot on the top of an old man's thick crown of hair. When I travel—and this started when I was nine years old—I always end up in the same locale. The actual spot on the planet Earth stays the same; just what is on it is different. In the future, this is the location of my neighborhood.

I lifted off a thatch of twigs to expose a deep hole; one I had proudly dug myself having *borrowed* a shovel from a neighboring farm. Inside was a hatchet, spotty with rust, a piece of flint, a rugged slingshot and two musky smelling burlap bags, which I pulled out, one at a time. The first had food—dried beef, raisins and a jar of well water. I opened the jar, took a drink and grimaced. Stale. The second bag had clothing: a long ivory cotton dress with tiny bluebells hand stitched in a scattered pattern, ladies boots that looked like figure skates with the blades off, a pair of trousers, a pair of men's boots, (yes, my feet were big enough to wear men's) and a boy's cap. I'd *borrowed* these during various trips, and hoarded them away for the "future."

A stumpy, fallen log, green with moss and partially hollowed out by ants, served as a bench. I rested against it, laying Nate's ball on the ground. I stared at it hypnotically, until I was lulled into a deep daydream, back to the football field at Cambridge High. This time I did everything right.

Nate says, *Good catch*, his eyes admiring me and my obvious, though previously hidden, athletic ability. I say, *Thanks*, and smile back with confidence, my hair perfectly tamed and my jeans fitting me exceptionally well. And most importantly, I give the ball back, offering it like a prize, our fingers lightly brushing in the pass. Nate throws it far and long, glancing back to see if I am still watching him.

I screamed. A garter snake had slithered over my hand. I jumped to my feet and did a little impromptu rain dance. I wasn't even afraid of garter snakes, it just startled me. My heart settled back to normal speed and I shook my head, trying to clear it. *Focus, Casey.* Sometimes it was difficult separating my two crazy worlds. I so didn't feel like being here in my alternate universe, the year 1860.

I put on the trousers. Fortunately, the fashion for boys in the nineteenth century was loose and baggy, so no need to lie flat on my back to wrestle with a zipper (which wasn't invented yet, anyway). Picking up Nate's ball, I tucked it securely under my shirt. I had to make sure the ball came home with me when I went. It served a second useful purpose, adding the illusion of boyish thickness to my waistline. A bit of twine made for a functional belt.

Shoot. The pant legs ended at my ankles. Okay, I forgot to add to my list of imperfections, (chronic bad hair days, the time travel thing, paralyzing crush on a way unobtainable hottie) that I'm also overly tall. Not graceful catwalk model tall or academy award winner beauty tall. More like ostrich tall. Without the feathers. Long limbs with knobby knees and elbows.

I pushed my hair behind my ears and into the cap. I hadn't picked up the habit of wearing make-up because a) a bare face aided me in my attempts to blend in and b) it was a liability to me when I traveled and wanted to pass myself off as a boy. I practiced at lowering my voice: Hello, my name is Casey.

I cleaned up my stash and worked to wipe out the evidence of a human visitation. I decided to head for the Watson farm, to see if Willie Watson would hire me again. It was grunt work, cows and chickens and the like, but it gave me a way to make a bit of money and get food. There were also a ton of kids and I could easily get lost in the mix.

At the main road I turned east towards Boston. Mid autumn leaves shook in the cool breeze causing goose bumps to pop up on my arms in defense of the chill. I rubbed them vigorously with my long fingers. Behind me I heard the growing rhythmic clip-clop of a single horse and cart. A young man with a mass of red, curly hair came to a stop at my side, stirring up a minor cloud of dust. I recognized him despite that fact he had filled out since the last time I'd seen him and unfamiliar stubble now shadowed his face. It was Willie Watson.

"Can I offer you a lift?" he said.

It was show time. I lowered my voice. "Willie?"

"Casey?"

"Yeah, it's me."

He cupped his hands over his eyes to block the sun. "I hardly recognized you. You've gotten so tall."

"I've heard."

"Where you off to?"

I shifted my weight, in a manly (I hoped) way. "Well actually, I was wondering if I could work for you again."

Willie nodded. "We can always use an extra hand. Get in."

I shared the back of the cart with a bale of hay and a little goat with a gray beard. Willie snapped the reins, the initial thrust tossing me to the back end of the cart where I settled in for the ride. I was happy to get out of the long walk to the Watsons' farm, not too happy about hitching a ride with a goat. It sensed my discomfort and immediately reached over to nibble on my shirt. I swatted the air between us. "Back off!"

Willie called over his shoulder. "What happened to you? You just took off last time without saying anything."

I had my cover story ready. "I had to get back to Springfield. Family stuff. But my ma just had number thirteen so Pa sent me out to work again."

"Aye, I understand. My own mother is kept to her room with number ten."

I'd first met Willie when we were both twelve. He'd caught me stealing eggs from their chicken coop. Not my finest moment, I admit, but I plead desperation, driven to petty theft due to the fact that I had crossed off day eight in the past. Up until then, my trips had usually only lasted a couple days, but that summer things changed. Hungry and panicked, I'd thought I was stuck in the past forever, never to return home, never to see my parents or my younger brother, Timothy, ever again. I'd crept like a fox at dawn to the nearest farm.

Thankfully, that was the Watson farm, and the Watsons had turned out to be the nicest and kindest people I'd ever met. Anyway, Willie had caught me with my hand in the cookie jar, so to speak. "You gonna eat those raw?" he'd said. I hadn't thought about that. I'd shrugged, too stunned and frightened to say anything of intelligence. "We have hotcakes in the kitchen, you can come for breakfast." The thought of eating with all those Watsons was just too scary. My face must've reflected that, since Willie went on to say, "That's okay, I'll bring you some. Wait for me on the dock." I'd nodded and watched in silence as Willie gathered the eggs before leaving.

I'd made my way to the small lake situated in the middle of the Watson farm, thinking that I was either going to get a yummy breakfast or Willie was going to return with a gun and take me to the jail house. He'd showed up with breakfast.

"Thanks," I'd said. Willie's voice hadn't yet changed so he didn't think twice about my high-pitched squeakiness. I ate the warm and sticky pancakes with my dirty, bare hands. I'd tried to imagine what I looked like to Willie. I hadn't showered in ten days, and my hair was grimy and in hysterics. Just like those kids in Lord of the Flies after a few weeks without parents to boss them around. He never snitched on me about my chicken house raid and got me a job pitching hay. I'd stayed in the past for a full three weeks, and from that point on the "rules" of time travel had altered. Now, I never knew how long I'd be gone.

We rode the rest of the way to the farm in silence. Well, except for the goat, ba-aa-ing and nipping at my pant legs.

I rubbed my butt when we arrived, though the bumpy ride was appreciated by both me and the goat.

"I could use help milking the cows and keeping the barn clean," Willie said, pointing to the prominent red out-building behind the stately family home. "You can sleep in the loft, like last time," he added. I strutted away, concentrating on my gait, mimicking my brother's boyish walk. Swiveling hips would get me into big trouble. Times like this made me thankful for my poached egg sized breasts. Just call me *Mr.* Casey.

Someone watched me walk across the yard. Of course, there were plenty of people around, other workers, Watson kids playing tag, but I felt his eyes on me. Cobbs. He was shorter than me now, but beefy like a boxer with a round beer belly popping out. His face was pink and shiny and his dark beady eyes scanned my body.

Ew, what a perv. *I'm a boy, weirdo!* Or could he tell I wasn't? Did he remember me from before? Either way he was a creeper. I let my gaze fall to the ground and kept walking, away from the barn. When I was sure Cobbs was out of sight I circled back and slipped into the barn, climbing the ladder to the loft. I hid in the pokey straw and even though it was only dusk, I immediately fell asleep.

. . .

THE TINY IRRITATING saw of a mosquito buzzed near my face, and I flapped my hands dramatically. A rooster crowed and I sighed, disappointed I was still in the past. Not that I would travel in the night. I never traveled while sleeping. Ever. Didn't know why. Some kind of time travel law.

And I was hungry. Better go milk me some cows and earn my breakfast. A dozen Jersey cows lined up in a row. Grabbing a tin pail and wooden stool, I settled in under Betsy One. I called them all Betsy: Betsy One through Thirteen.

Willie joined me. "Mornin', Casey." He grabbed a short three-legged stool like the one I sat on, and plopped a pail under Betsy Three. It had been a while since I'd had to milk a cow, and honestly, I never did get the hang of it. First of all, cow teats are like short slippery ropes. Kind of gross to touch. And you have to pull on them just so, sort of a milk-releasing-rhythm. The cows get fully irritated when you don't get it right.

Thwap, thwap, thwap. The sound of milk shooting into a metal pail. Unfortunately, not my pail. Willie was showing me up.

I peeked around the back end of Betsy One, spying on Willie's Olympic cow milking performance. Betsy One didn't like my peering around her rear end, and whacked me hard with her tail. Kind of like getting smacked with a bull whip, but one covered in fur.

"Ouch!"

"You okay, Casey?" Willie called.

"Uh, yeah, fine." I mimicked Willie's timing, one, two, three, four, and thankfully the milk started to shoot out.

By the time I finished my fifth cow, (meaning Willie whipped my butt by milking eight), my forearms burned and throbbed like mad. We carried the pails to the kitchen where the Watson kids poured the milk into jars so the older boys could make deliveries in the neighborhood.

The eldest Watson kid, Sara, oversaw the whole operation. Her red hair was parted down the center and two braids close to her face looped up like crimson handles. Though fashionable for this century, not a very becoming look as far as I was concerned. It seemed like she had a large lampshade under her skirt, the way it spread out at the bottom, and since women didn't normally wear hoops while working at home, I assumed that she must be about to go out. When she saw me, she propped her hands upon her waist.

"Willie," she called. "Who do we have here?" She didn't remember me because Willie, and his father when he was around, took responsibility for farm staff. She, when her mother was ill or with child, controlled the kitchen and house staff.

"Ah, you remember Casey Donovan? He's worked here before."

"Really? I don't recall." Sara pinched her eyebrows together. Then she called out, "Duncan, Josephine, Charlotte, Abigail, Jonathon!" A collection of kids with either curly red or brunette hair entered the room.

With the guidance of a stout and bright faced woman named Missy, they went to work bottling the milk, careful not to get knocked to the ground by Sara's hoop skirt.

Willie left and I turned to follow, but she cleared her throat, stopping me. I waited to be dismissed, but she held my gaze. She got right to the point. "How old are you?"

"Uh, almost sixteen."

"Do you shave, Casey?"

"Uh," My hand jumped to my chin. "Sometimes. I'm a late bloomer. It runs in my family."

"I dare say. Did you spend the night in the loft?"

"Yes."

"Alone?"

"I think so. I fell asleep shortly after my arrival yesterday. I don't remember seeing anyone else."

"That's a relief," she said.

"Why is that?"

She removed her apron and smoothed out her skirt. Then she looked me straight in the eye. "Because Casey Donovan, I believe that you are a girl as surely as I am one."

TWO

MY COVER WAS BLOWN. I'd always expected this would happen someday—just not so soon. Sara motioned for me to follow her across the kitchen. Though bigger than most nineteenth century kitchens, it obviously lacked modern appliances and conveniences. No fridge or microwave, though there was a stove. It was an over-sized, cast iron, wood burning fancy looking thing. Water came from a pump in the yard.

The Watson house was bigger than most farm houses. Its large entry with nice oak doors opened up to a staircase with a run of mosaic carpeting down the middle. You could tell that, whatever it was that Mr. Watson did when he went away, he made money doing it.

I followed Sara up the stairs and down a hallway, until she opened the door to a bedroom that obviously belonged to her and at least one sister. Two beds with lacy canopies filled the corners of the room. An ornate wooden vanity desk with an oval mirror sat in between them, brushes and combs with pearl-like handles lay elegantly on top.

She turned around sharply and crossed her arms. "Please explain."

"Well, I, uh, you see, my family is very large and come upon hard times, and I, uh, needed to seek work to help out, so because, of course, it's not prudent to travel alone as a girl, I thought I should dress in my brother's clothes...."

Sara put a hand up, rescuing me from my rambling. "I understand. You are making the most of a difficult situation, and I respect that. However, it is highly inappropriate for you to work alone with the men, and so from this moment on you shall assist me in the house."

She walked to the wardrobe on the opposite end of the room and fished through a row of dresses, choosing one. "I will find you suitable clothing. There's plenty of work for another woman around here. Indeed, your arrival is timely. With Mother bed-resting and Father off to London, there is plenty to do."

She eyed my figure. "Here, this should be fine, though you are rather tall. Just hike the slip down a couple inches." She tossed me a pair of shoes and I smiled. She had big feet, too.

"I'll leave you to get dressed," Sara said. "Meet me in the kitchen when you're ready. Oh, and Casey isn't suitable for a young lady. We'll call you Cassandra."

Cassandra. That was a mouthful. But I wasn't about to argue with Sara Watson.

The dress was soft to the touch and I pressed it against myself as I studied my image in the mirror. I couldn't help but break into a waltz and dance with the dress around the room.

I suddenly felt dizzy. I reached for the back of the vanity chair and let the dress drop onto the seat. I wasn't about to go anywhere with Sara. I was about to exit stage right. Just in time I remembered to grab Nate's ball from my waistband.

I fell into a dizzying flash of white light and in a split second I was back—on the school field with Lucinda at my side and Nate right in front of me. They had no idea about my recent adventure. I was back in my regular clothes and the only change in my appearance, I knew, were the dark circles under my eyes that always appeared after I traveled. All they saw was me having just made a spectacular catch.

Nate's expression morphed from congratulatory to perplexed in two seconds flat. Why, when I finally got to be this close to him, did I have to look like crap?

But he wasn't looking at my face. He was looking at my hands, or rather, at the deflated object in my hands.

"What happened to my ball?"

I hate my life!

"Man!" Nate took the ball from me and examined the flattened mess. "There's a hole right through Tom Brady!"

"I just caught it," I whimpered.

All Nate's friends surrounded me, and then to make matters infinitely worse, Jessica Fuller and her gaggle of cheerleaders pushed through. Jessica Fuller, aka Nate's girlfriend, was a strawberry blond beauty queen with a great big toothy smile. She was Nate's one flaw, which I attributed to Jessica's bewitching deceitfulness and chose to ignore. Nate was new to Cambridge High, having moved from Toronto just last year, and Jessica had gotten her artificial claws into him before he could see what was coming.

"Ew!" She looked at me like I had just eaten a worm.

Her eyes squished into small holes, and she pursed her puffy lips together. She wouldn't stop staring. It was like she was seeing me for the very first time, like a pimple that appears overnight. A miniature irrigation system embedded under my skin suddenly sprayed in each armpit.

"Casey?" Lucinda's eyes were wide with near panic. "Are you okay?"

I cleared my throat. "I, uh, need to go." Like the Red Sea parting, the football players and cheerleaders moved. With my sweaty armpits and black ringed eyes, I slunk away. Lucinda, because she was a great best friend, ran after me.

"Casey?" Her eyes scanned my face; the dark rings were a big giveaway. "You tripped?"

Trip was our slang for time travel. She was the only other person on the face of the earth that knew about my secret life.

This was because I'd accidentally taken Lucinda back once. That was how I'd learned about the dangers of skin to skin contact. We were ten, playing tag in the back yard. The air had been moist and warm, and we'd just finish drinking homemade lemonade. I'd tagged her saying, "you're it" and off we went, down a spinning bright ride, but believe me, it was no Disney-land. It was the first time Lucinda had ever spent the night away from home. Also the first time she had to spend the night outside. No tent, no nothing. She freaked out so much she didn't speak to me for a week afterwards. I apologized, explained to her that it didn't happen very often, and promised that it would never happen to her again. She just couldn't touch my skin.

And neither could anyone else. These were terms she could live with. Eventually.

"That was so humiliating!" I moaned.

"But are you okay?"

"Define okay." Lucinda eyeball scanned me. "Well, you're in one piece. How long were you gone?"

"Two days. Oh, Lucinda! When I imagined Nate Mackenzie finally noticing me, it wasn't like this!"

Lucinda just nodded her head in sympathy. "Tomorrow is another day." She flipped her long dark hair over her shoulder. "Everyone will have forgotten all about it by then."

"Nice try, Luce. I wrecked Nate Mackenzie's ball."

"Um, yeah, that's unfortunate."

Understatement of the year! We parted ways when my bus arrived. I leaned my head against the window of the first available seat, closed my eyes and cruelly let the incident replay on the theater screen of my mind. Over and over. Each time the disgust I saw on Nate's and Jessica's faces grew, until practically gremlin-like.

Why did that have to happen to me? Why couldn't I just be normal? I felt sick, a rock sitting heavy and hard in my stomach. When I got home, I checked all the rooms in the house, calling for my mom and Timothy.

Once I was completely certain that I was home alone, I shut myself in my bedroom, flopped on my bed and screamed into my pillow. I was a freak, a monster, an alien.

The only solution, I decided in that weak moment, was to quit school. So what if I was a sophomore still two months away from my sixteenth birthday?

Maybe I could do night school. Small classes, no jocks to distract me or cheerleaders to intimidate me. When I finally screamed myself out, I found that I felt a bit better. I put on my comfort clothes, SpongeBob Squarepants pajamas and monkey slippers, and shuffled downstairs to the sofa and the remote control.

I almost succeeded in pushing Nate out of my mind. After watching a series of mind numbing infomercials, I snapped out of my dark mood and came to my senses. Quitting school was a dumb idea, and besides I suddenly had a better one. Instead of loving Nate, I would hate him. Yes, Hate Nate Mackenzie. And that silly, stupid girlfriend of his, too. Suddenly, I felt lots better.

The next day, I went to school, more determined than ever to stay on the down low. Must avoid Nate. Must avoid Nate.

Unfortunately, his evil girlfriend cornered me after first class. "I remember you," she said. Yeah, duh. My public humiliation was just yesterday. So much for Lucinda's prediction that everyone would forget about it. "You're one of those losers who watches the football practices after school."

Was she saying that everyone who watches the practices after school is a loser? My silence didn't shut her up.

"You have a crush on Nate, don't you?"

Finally, I found my tongue. "I do not." In fact, I wanted to say, I now officially hate him.

"I can tell, you know. The way you and your sorry little friend stare at him all the time."

First of all, Lucinda wasn't sorry and she didn't have a crush on Nate, even though she agreed that he was hot. Second of all, I couldn't disagree with the last part about staring at him all the time, but I was determined to change.

"We stare at all the guys."

"He's mine. You stay away."

"Yeah, sure." I maneuvered away from her and her peeps. "He's all yours."

"And don't forget that." She added loudly, so all her little cheerleader peons could hear and laugh. "You'll never be good enough for Nate Mackenzie."

Did I mention how they laughed? Must avoid Nate and Jessica. Must avoid Nate and Jessica.

But now I had English, which, because Nate sat two seats in front of me, made a dizzying drop from my favorite class to my absolute worst class. I used to think that it was fate that put us both in the same English class. Nate, a senior, was in an English 11 class because his courses got mixed up when he moved here from Canada. I was in this class as a sophomore because the Advanced Sophomore English course was full, and so the powers that be bumped me up. Now I thought it was a curse.

My worries about how to avoid Nate were unnecessary, since he didn't look at me once. Everything was back to normal. Normal meaning that he didn't even register my presence but all my senses were completely and totally ignited. Hating Nate would take some work.

Lucinda was in line at the cafeteria and waved me over when she saw me walk in. We hadn't talked since the incident. "I texted you," Lucinda whined.

"Shush." I pressed my finger to my lips in warning, motioning with my eyebrows that a certain someone was in the near vicinity. "Not so loud."

"Oh, my bad." She lowered her voice, "It's just that I was worried about you."

Fortunately we arrived at the front of the line and had to stop talking while the café worker poured the hot meal, I think it was chili, onto the plate. Lucinda, who was average in height, went first and then me, the lumbering giant. At least that's how I felt next to her.

We met up again at our usual table, chosen so we could get a good look at the guys at the jock table. Not that we were completely boy crazy; we did retain our sanity slash dignity for, say, 75% of the day, but at lunch and after school practices, why not enjoy the scenery? An almost undecipherable musical tune came from Lucinda's bag. Her cell phone. Lucinda could hear like a dog. With a hand-is-quicker-than-the-eye expertise she had it opened and hidden under a sheath of her long hair.

"My sister," she mouthed, then started talking in wildfire fast Portuguese.

I took a bite of the chili. Not great but not bad either for caf food. I snatched the opportunity with Lucinda occupied to glance furtively around the cafeteria. I saw Nate with his friends at the jock table, but I only let my eyes linger for a nanosecond.

Lucinda snapped her phone shut, "So, like, what exactly happened yesterday?" She flung her long black hair and waited.

I envied Lucinda's hair. It was so straight and shiny. "You already know, I tripped."

"Yeah, but before that. You jumped up and caught his ball."

A loud commotion from the middle of the room distracted us.

Someone had dropped their tray, splattering chili all over the floor. It looked like vomit. From the cries of "ew" and "gross," I knew I wasn't alone in thinking it. Jessica made a big point of walking a wide circle around it, shouting, "That's disgusting!" I watched for Nate's reaction. He only gave it (and her) his attention for a moment before returning to a loud and animated conversation with Tyson and Josh about last night's game on TV. Tyson's black biceps flexed as he demonstrated a throw. Josh's curly red hair seemed to spring with excitement. Must've been some game.

Jessica wasn't the type who liked to share the spotlight. With Nate pre-occupied, she saddled up beside Craig Kellerman, and shamelessly flirted with him even though he was a sophomore.

"Why does Nate put up with that?" I said to Lucinda.

"She's just trying to make him jealous so he'll pay more attention to her."

A large and colorful new poster hung on the wall near our table. I caught Lucinda's eyes darting towards it repeatedly. "What's up?"

"The Fall Dance is in two weeks," said Lucinda.

With a mouthful of chili I said, "Yeah, so what?"

"I think we should go."

I examined her dark eyes and wondered if she'd gone mad. "We never go to dances." I sipped a bit of soda.

"But, this is our last chance."

Did I miss something? "Our last chance for what?"

"It's our last chance to practice for, like, the Junior Prom."

I raised an eyebrow. "I wasn't exactly planning on going to that." I took another bite.

"Casey," Lucinda wiped her mouth with a napkin. "If we don't practice for the Junior Prom we won't know what to do at THE Prom."

"So, you want to go to the Fall Dance in order to practice for the Junior Prom in order to practice for THE Prom?" Lucinda nodded with a big wide smile. "But, THE Prom's still two years away and I probably won't go to it anyway."

Lucinda blew her bangs out of her eyes. "You totally have to go to THE Prom. It's like a rite of passage or something. The Fall Dance is a chance to learn, to see how it's done." She pulled a compact mirror out of her purse and checked her teeth. "Also, we don't want to screw up due to ignorance at the Junior Prom and thus screw up at THE Prom."

She had been thinking about this. A lot. "Okay. So, this is sort of a fact finding mission."

"Yes, totally."

"No actual dancing?"

"Of course not." Lucinda shuddered.

"I don't know." I put all my garbage on my tray. "It sounds risky."

Lucinda reached into her purse and pulled out two strips of thin, shiny cardboard.

"You already bought tickets?" I said through clenched teeth.

"Casey," Lucinda cocked her head and said gently. "It will be fun."

She thought it would be fun. I thought it would be a nightmare.

THREE

IT WAS WEDNESDAY. Wednesday was officially mean girl day. So was Thursday, and Friday and every other day of the week, because I was on Jessica's hit list. Which meant whispers and giggles as I passed by in the hall. Disparaging comments about my wild hair. If I hadn't had my nose in my biology textbook, I would have heard her coming.

"Move, people. Move it." Jessica's cheerleader trained voice pitched through the hall. Instead of floating past me like she usually did, she and her posse stopped to gawk. "Looky here," Jessica said, popping bubble gum. "A weather vane. How's the air up there?"

I looked down on her red/blond head, her naturally wavy locks mercilessly hot ironed into sheets. "Suddenly cooler," I said.

"You mean, hotter." She flicked her bangs off her face."Right, girls?" The posse laughed. "Nice shirt, Casey." I peered down at the 725 logo on my brown long sleeved T-shirt. "Isn't that from WAL-MART?" Her girls giggled. They all dressed like Jessica—Lululemon hoodies in every pastel color of the rainbow, Guess miniskirts and Ugg boots.

"Do you need something, Jessica?" I said. "Tutoring?" It was rumored that when Jessica had first heard that Nate was from Canada, she'd asked him where he'd learned English. *Parlez-vous francais*, anyone?

"I don't need anything from you, flag pole. Oh, there's Nate." I glanced over and saw Nate watching us from the door of the science lab. How long had he been standing there? Jessica ran to him, throwing her arms around his waist. He didn't stop looking at me, even as he guided her into class. Was he mocking me?

It hadn't dawned on me during the Fall Dance discussion that to go to the dance meant having to wear a dress. Not that I had problems with dresses; I owned a trendy skirt that I sometimes wore on weekends. But I'd made a career out of staying under the radar, something I had failed at miserably the last few days, and dress wearing was absolutely "radar" worthy. That, along with the necessary accompanying makeup and fancy hair, definitely didn't fit in with my commitment to blandness and blending in. Unfortunately, there wasn't much I could do, except stay away from reds and satins, seeing as I'd already agreed to go.

Saturday was dress shopping day. Mom was already up drinking coffee in the living room flipping between the news channel and the home design network. Magazines on kitchens, bathrooms, living rooms, outdoor space, you name it, anything that can be made over, were found in stacks in most rooms of our house. Paint samples were spread out like a fan on our table, along with fabric samples and short wooden and metal blinds samples of every color. Tucked next to them was a bulkier suitcase sized sampler with swaths of carpet choices. The collection had turned into a small mountain since Mom had gone back to work.

I sat beside her with my bowl of cereal and said between mouthfuls, "I'm going into Boston with Lucinda today."

Mom muted the television. "What for?"

"Dress shopping. Lucinda has this crazy idea about going to the Fall Dance."

Mom's expression turned serious. "You're going to a dance?"

I hedged. "Only because Lucinda talked me into it. It's research for THE Prom, still eons away."

"Do you want me to come?" Mom suddenly looked excited. "I should help you pick out your dress for your first dance."

That didn't go the way I'd thought. "It's really not a big deal, Mom. I'm actually just going to help Lucinda pick out a dress."

Mom's shoulders slumped a bit. I felt terrible, but Lucinda wasn't bringing her mother and it would be weird for me to bring mine.

"You can help me pick out my Prom dress, Mom. I promise. Okay?"

Mom shrugged off her disappointment. "Okay, you have fun, then." She stood and gave me a soft smile. She was shorter than me, which I only really noticed when we hugged. She had blond hair cut stylishly short and not curly. The only thing I inherited from my mom was her fair skin and hazel eyes. "You can show me what you bought later," she added before heading to the kitchen for a refill.

I met Lucinda at the train, just in time to catch the red line subway to the Downtown Crossing station. When we emerged, we were in the middle of Boston. Downtown Crossing was a pedestrian mall, and a palette for the senses: pungent smells from the hot dog vendors, boom boxes blasting as athletes "danced" with their basketballs, and the chatter of many languages.

"Ooh, I love coming into Boston!" Lucinda was almost glassy-eyed as we stumbled along the cobblestone walkway, peering in the shops, stopping every few seconds to admire some item of clothing or accessory in a window.

"Looove that top!" Lucinda's never quite herself when shopping.

"It's nice, Luce," I said. After dipping into numerous boutiques we couldn't afford, I begged Lucinda to please just pick a place. Shopping was fun for some, but for me it was laborious. Thankfully, Lucinda finally came to her senses and picked Filenes Basement. At least that was a place where I stood a chance at finding something I could afford. We weren't alone. Could it be that every teenage girl in Metro Boston was dress shopping at this very hour? All at Filenes? It was shoulder to shoulder, which in any circumstance was nerve wracking. I needed space. I tugged nervously on my long sleeves.

"Hey, can we pick it up here? I'm starting to feel claustrophobic."

Lucinda took charge. "Check this rack out." She selected a number of dresses and thrust them at me. Then her cell rang and she answered it, wandering off to converse in Portuguese. At least I could be alone in the changing room.

I breathed deeply for a few minutes before stripping down. I decided on the first one. Why not? Why go through the agony of pulling countless dresses on and off, over my head. I knew what static did to my hair. Hello, Afro.

Mine was yellow. No, Lucinda corrected me, *saffron*. It was a plain princess style dress with narrow pleats gathering under my chest, a low-ish neckline and a hem just long enough to conceal my knobby knees.

"You look great," Lucinda said when I showed it off. "Oh, come on," I said.

"It's true. That color looks really nice with your hair and eyes. It's just perfect for your skin tone."

Perfect for my skin tone? "Well, thanks. Does it make me look tall?"

Lucinda tilted her head. "But, you are tall."

"I know, but do these vertical pleats add to my tallness?"

"Casey, it looks good on you." Lucinda chose blue and I

thought she looked stunning. Our dresses would be perfect for standing around in a large, dark, cavernous room for a whole night of watching other people dance. Mission happily accomplished.

Well, almost happily. Just as we approached the exit I spotted Nate. What was he doing here? Seeing him outside of the context of school was weird, though any context seemed to have the same effect on me. Dry throat, butterflies in my stomach, the urge to squeal.

I tried to make a smooth maneuver out of his line of vision, but instead ran directly into a rack of blouses, almost knocking it over. He saw me. Of course he saw me! The whole store stopped to observe. His eyes didn't flick away. *Okay, I'm a train wreck, you don't have to stare.*

He finally looked back at what he was watching before—Jessica presenting a pretty ivory dress. At first, she seemed startled to see me but then she grinned her evil grin. What? Did she think she was getting married to him? It looked like a dumb wedding dress. I really hoped she didn't pick that one.

A wave of dizziness smacked me as I tried to stand. Then a flash of bright light.

I was nine years old the first time it happened. Mom was tucking me in and had just turned out the lights. The red digital numbers on my clock read 8:31. Like a lot of kids, I was afraid of the dark and monsters under the bed, and I had, without my parents knowing, watched a scary B movie that afternoon. Every time Mom had checked in on me, I quickly clicked the remote to switch to the family channel. So, as soon as Mom closed my bedroom door and left me in the dark, I panicked. I lost my breath, felt dizzy and fell into the brightness.

And yes, I freaked out. But, you can only do so much crying and screaming in the middle of a dense forest, which I figured out later, was the same piece of land my house had eventually been built on. To make matters worse, it was raining and by the time I had finished my emotional breakdown, my PJs were soaked. I'd finally gotten my wits about me and spotted a large tree with a hole worn out on the side, and crouched in it, out of the rain. I spent the whole night shivering, scared out of my mind.

The next morning the sun shone brightly, so I removed my PJs and set them out on a rock to dry. Basking in the sun had warmed me up, but I was hungry. I searched around for food wearing only underpants. I must have looked like the Jungle Book boy with my nine year old, prepubescent body, and my shorter dark curly hair. Eventually, I found some berries and ate them without considering that they could be poisonous. I've since done my homework, so I know, and fortunately those berries were fine and I didn't get sick.

I didn't know what triggered the trip back. Probably emotional and physical fatigue. I felt dizzy, but nothing happened right away, not like when I traveled from the present to the past.

I headed back to where I'd left my PJs, but couldn't find them. I was lost! However, it turned out I didn't need to worry about that. I fell into the tunnel of light and the next thing I knew, I was in my bed, with my PJs on, and my mother was just closing the door behind her. I looked at the clock—8:31. No time had gone by at all!

But now, here, I was whirling through the light in downtown Boston. Until this trip, I'd always traveled near my home in Cambridge, and similarly, near my stash and the Watson Farm. This was the first time I'd traveled while hanging out in Boston. I didn't know why. Nothing had ever triggered it before. I blamed it on Nate Mackenzie and the way he affected my pulse. At any rate, I was in foreign waters, so to speak. Actually, I was in some-one's little wooden shack.

A dirty faced woman with a dirty long dress and a dirty apron to match was staring wide eyed at me. I could tell I was doing the same back at her. Then her eyes narrowed and she practically hissed. "Get ye out of me house, ya thievin'...laddie? Lassie? What are ye anyway?"

I didn't hang around to answer. I dashed out the door and onto a dusty street, narrowly missing getting run over by a horse and buggy. The lady didn't let my intrusion go. I could hear her shouting, "Thief, thief!" as I dashed away. I couldn't imagine what she thought I had taken. It didn't look like she had anything worth stealing.

I darted through the crowds, hoping to get out of sight before anyone could seize me. I shuddered at the thought of being arrested, and there was no way I could explain the way I looked— blue jeans, T-shirt, and long, out of control hair.

I turned a sharp corner and found myself in a dimly lit alley. A large rain barrel sat up against the building and I ducked in behind it. I didn't let myself breathe until I was certain I had not been followed. Thankfully, all the pedestrians continued walking past me, without taking a single interest in what was down the alley. Once I caught my breath, I took in my surroundings. My eyes had adjusted to the dimness and I was rewarded with a line of laundry hanging a short ways behind me.

I snagged a buttoned-down stained, white shirt, and shimmied on a pair of men's trousers on top of my jeans. A quick scour of the trash on the ground produced a piece of twine. I tied my hair back into a low ponytail and stuffed it into the back of the shirt.

Keeping my eyes to the ground, I stepped into the flow of foot traffic and headed towards Longfellow Bridge. Which turned out to be a long way away. After a while, my legs ached, my head hurt and I was dying of thirst. I had to find a way to speed up my journey. When I got close to the bridge I spotted a carriage, the fancy kind with trims and a bumper. I ran behind it, grabbed on and pulled myself up. These were the days before shocks and efficient suspension systems. Thin wooden wheels riding on cobblestones and gravel rattled my ribcage. I held on tight.

People we passed by hooted and hollered at me; some thinking that hitching a ride like that was cheap thing to do, and others cheering me on, like a hero. I just kept my head down, glad that the large team of horses made a ton of noise with their clip-clopping and whinnying, and that the carriage didn't have any rear view mirrors. It came to a stop in Lexington. I hopped off and scooted into the neighboring forest. I wasn't home free yet, but at least I knew how to get to the Watson's from here.

Finally, I got to the property. I stopped at the water pump and filled my gullet. Cold water never felt so good! I didn't even care that I was soaking myself. After I had enough to drink, I gave my face a good scrub. Then I headed to the house.

Time passes differently in the past and I guessed a month or so had passed for the Watsons since I'd caught Nate's ball, so I wasn't so sure how Sara would take my sudden reappearance, but I had no other options than to hope that Sara would give me another chance.

Sara scowled when she saw me. "You're back." A statement, not a question. I nodded.

"I wish to ask your forgiveness, ma'am, for my bad manners, leaving so suddenly as I did." I could hear myself slipping into the speech patterns of the time. Another survival tactic I'd picked up along the way. "I was afraid. I'm hoping you will give me a second chance. I'm still in need of honest work."

She stared at me like I was a new project. "I suppose there was no real harm done." She studied me for a moment, then sighed. "Besides, you look like you could use some help." I was certain I looked a complete and total mess. I was sweaty and dust-covered, and still dressed like a boy. Sara led me back upstairs, removed the same dress and shoes from the closet then squinted at me before leaving. I imagined her standing guard on the other side of the door. The first thing I did was peel off my clothes and sponge bath with the tepid water in the pitcher and basin on the dresser—ever so happy to see a bar of soap.

ONCE DRESSED, I carefully opened the door. Sara was nowhere in sight. I tentatively tackled the steps with my heels, grateful for the railing to steady me. I found Sara in the kitchen, and when she saw me, her jaw dropped. "My word, Cassandra. I'd never have recognized you."

I must've cleaned up nice, because for the first time, Sara smiled. There was a heady, yummy scent coming from the room, and my stomach growled loudly. Very unladylike!

"Missy," Sara said to the ruddy-faced, stout helper in the kitchen. "Please give our guest something to eat."

Sara watched me as I ate a slice of warm, buttered bread— home made and an inch thick—and sipped on soup that was also really tasty. I hadn't realized how long it had been since I'd eaten and I was famished. But still, with this getup on, I forced myself to maintain the table manners my mother had taught me. Sara noticed, too.

"I see, Cassandra, that you are well-bred. Your manners and behavior seem inconsistent with your presentation earlier. I am perplexed."

"Miss Watson," I started.

"Please, call me Sara."

"Sara," I continued, "even though my family has suffered hard times, my mother taught her children manners."

"How happy for you," Sara said. "And apparently you were availed of an education as well? Can you read?"

"Yes." She paused, and then seemed to come to a decision.

"I'm going to the bookstore, presently. Would you like to accompany me?"

More than a bit surprised by her invitation, I nodded. "I'd like that." Besides, what else was I going to do? After I finished my meal, Sara ushered me back upstairs, where she presented me with a hoop underskirt and a bonnet.

"Meet me at the front door when you are ready."

I put on the big hoop skirt, and almost burst out laughing. How on earth was a woman to function efficiently when her clothing virtually pushed her two feet away from the very thing she was trying to grasp?

Sara started speaking the moment I entered the foyer. "Mr. Kelsey is at the bookstore most days. I want him to see that though he and those other buffoons won't permit us to attend university, they can't stop us girls from learning."

She handed me a shawl and a parasol. I felt like a little girl playing dress up. She had a driver take us by carriage into Boston. I found it more than odd to be going back into the city so soon, this time riding in the carriage and dressed like a lady. Could this day get any stranger?

At least this time I could take in the scenery in comfort. I stared out the window. No automobiles, no trains, no Mass Pike. This was the part that really messed with my head. I had been here in my time just this morning, shopping with Lucinda at Filenes! Nate had been there too, and his dumb girlfriend. Now Filenes didn't even exist and there were far fewer buildings. It felt like a movie set.

Lots of horses, too, which also translated into lots of horse dung. The air in the city had a sour smell. The sewer was unmanaged, every chimney pumped out ash and smoke, and dirty children ran amuck, the effect of their once a week bath from a shared tub not lasting nearly long enough. The upper classes compensated by excessive use of perfume. After a while, my sniffing sensory just shut down.

I followed Sara into the Good Ol' Book Shoppe, stunned by the great and ancient literary works. I picked up a volume of *Gray's Anatomy, Descriptive and Surgical*. And here I thought Grey's Anatomy was just a TV Drama.

"Are you interested in medicine?" A masculine voice with a tinge of amusement said this. He was tall, (I always notice if a guy is taller than me), maybe in his late twenties, with dark eyes and hair. He wore a tailored suit, and had the confident smugness that came with having a lot of money. I glanced around to see if someone else was also perusing a medical journal. Nope. He must be talking to me.

"I'm not sure," I said. No need to commit either way. Though I didn't think medicine would be a good choice for a time traveler. Imagine giving someone a needle or stitches and taking off for a mid-appointment holiday to a destination a hundred and fifty some years away.

"Nursing is a fine profession for young women," he continued. "If, of course, teaching is not of interest."

Why was he talking to me? He stretched out his hand, "Excuse my manners. I'm Robert Willingsworth."

"Hello, I'm Case, uh, Cassandra Donovan." I shook his hand while nervously tucking a fly away hair under my bonnet. I was sure I looked horrid. I couldn't conceive why this man was still standing here, waiting for me to say something. Sara came to my rescue.

"Oh, Mr. Willingsworth! How do you do?"

"Miss Watson." He bowed slightly. "Always a pleasure."

"I see you have met my companion, Miss Donovan."

"Indeed." He turned to me. "Are you recently to town?"

"Yes, I arrived just this morning."

"My, your accent is endearing." Robert's eyes twinkled when he spoke and I blushed. Was he really flirting with me?

"From what town do you originate?"

"Springfield."

"Really? I once had the privilege of visiting Springfield. I don't recall the accent."

"Oh," I said quickly, "I'm actually from west of Springfield. A village no one's heard of." He studied me for a second and I worried that he would keep quizzing me. Then he smiled widely, splashing a set of large, straight teeth.

"Might I inquire, would you ladies allow me the good pleasure of a stroll? It's a beautiful day for a walk through the Common."

"What a delightful idea," Sara said. "Come along Cassandra, the fresh air will do us good."

He linked one arm through each of ours. The sun shone brightly and warmed the autumn air. Too bad these shoes were killing my feet!

Beacon Hill, Boston's most prestigious neighborhood, lined the north side of the generous park. A row of attractive, red brick townhouses trimmed with white lined the street with the State-house on the eastern end. Its famous gold dome was only made of copper in the year 1860, yet stunning all the same.

"Mr. Willingsworth is a recent graduate from Harvard, Cassandra."

"How nice." I racked my brain trying to recall the name Willingsworth from my history lessons. Though I excelled at the subject of American History, I drew a blank.

"What do you think of the coming election, Mr. Willingsworth?" Sara said.

"Oh, such conversation is not fitting for young ladies such as yourself and Miss Donovan." His little black mustache twitched.

I wasn't used to being talked down to and I couldn't help releasing a small 'hrumph' of air through my nose.

"Nonsense, Robert," Sara said. "I have a mind that can think."

"Very well. Lincoln hopes to win." He paused as if deciding whether to go on or not. I guess he decided we had brains enough to understand what he was about to say next, as he continued. "But, I fear he has alienated all the voters in the south due to his lack of, shall we say, enthusiasm regarding the institution of slavery."

"Slavery is barbaric," Sara said with feeling. I loved her feisty attitude and that she didn't let this guy intimidate her.

"Perhaps slavery is a bit extreme," Robert added, "but you must admit, they are great workers. Better than horses."

Better than horses? Mr. Willingsworth's charm had definitely worn off.

Sara lifted her chin. "If I could vote, I would vote Abraham Lincoln president of the United States of America."

"Voting is very serious business, Miss Watson."

"As is freedom." Even though I knew the best policy for me as a "visitor" was to just keep my mouth shut, I couldn't help myself. Robert and his 'I'm a man and therefore I'm better than you, a mere woman' attitude got on my nerves.

"Certainly, Miss Donovan," Robert conceded. "Freedom is a serious business as well. As are economics and rights of owners to their purchases."

"Even when the purchase refers to human beings?" I said with a tight smile.

"I meant no offense, Miss Donovan. I'm not necessarily stating my personal opinion."

"Blacks are persons and should be treated as such," Sara said.

I tried to keep it in, but it just popped out. "One day we may have a black president."Chew on that, Robert. He and Sara stopped, staring at me wide eyed.

Robert cracked a smile and then laughed. "Or we might have a woman for president! Miss Donovan, you are the most intriguing individual I have met in a long while."

We waited as a horse and buggy passed along a trail in front of us. "Mr. Willingsworth," Sara said, tugging on his arm. "Cassandra and I are attending the meeting at Faneuil Hall this afternoon."

We were?

"Abby Kelly Foster from Worcester is speaking," she added.

"The famed female abolitionist," Robert said, nodding. "Indeed, if you two beautiful ladies will be attending, I shall certainly be there as well." Robert said his farewells, holding eye contact with me a little bit too long for comfort. He promised to meet us in an hour.

Sara and I continued by foot to Quincy Market. "He seemed quite taken with you." Sara stared at the ground when she said this. I didn't think she was too happy about it, but I wouldn't insult her intelligence by denying it.

"For the life of me, I can't see why," I said.

"My dear Cassandra. Women who don't recognize their own beauty are the most attractive of them all." What the heck was she talking about? Unless opinionated, overly tall women with frizzy hair were considered beautiful in the nineteenth century.

"He's too old for me, anyway."

"Hardly. Girls our age marry men older than Mr. Willingsworth all the time. Cassandra, you say the most peculiar things."

I really should keep my mouth shut.

A crowd gathered on the steps of Faneuil Hall, a two story brick warehouse-like building with a weather vane sprouting from the middle of the roof. A farmers' market took up the whole ground floor which was filled with bustling shoppers and merchants. On the upper level an assembly hall was supported by several white pillars. An extra level of seating surrounded the room and increased the view of the podium. It was the only building of the three yet to be built which makes up the Quincy Market I knew. Fish stalls filled the lanes infusing the air with the tangy scent of the sea. I much preferred the sweet and savory aromas of the food court in my time as well as the festive air and craft shops.

Sara and I sat in the wooden chairs near the back of the first level of the Assembly Hall. Men and women occupied most of the seating, all murmuring with troubled expressions on their faces. I asked Sara about it.

"The city is much divided," she said. "Though we are a northern state, there are still many who think we should keep our noses out of the south. And others, like myself, think the problems of the south belong to us all."

Robert joined us as promised and, to my chagrin, chose the empty space next to me rather than the one beside Sara. I offered a sugary sweet ladylike smile, all the while comparing his features to Nate's. Eyes? Nate wins. Nose? Nate wins. Smile? Nate definitely wins.

Stop! What was the matter with me? Why do I keep forgetting that I Hate Nate? The meeting suddenly overflowed with abolitionists and anti-abolitionists from the south, each group with their placards yelling at each other across the aisles.

"Slavery is evil! Abolish the Fugitive Act!"

"Slavery is the American way! Keep your nose out of the South!"

Two men from opposing sides went to blows, like a modern day ice hockey fight. Cheers erupted from both sides, and I feared someone would get thrown over the balcony and onto the shoppers below.

"Miss Foster should be beginning shortly," Sara said, winding her face with her hand.

All the bodies and excitement in the room caused me to feel heated and flushed. I felt light-headed and took a deep breath. It wouldn't do for me to faint. They really had too many people in this room. There would be a stampede in an emergency. Did they have fire safety standards in place yet in 1860? I grew dizzy. Dizzy? Oh. Oh no, oh no, oh no. I had to get away from Sara and Robert, ASAP.

"Excuse me," I said, pushing my big hooped skirt past Robert, narrowly missing his nose. "I need some air."

"I'll assist you." Robert grabbed my arm, holding me back. In a panic, I shook him off.

"No, I'll be fine!" I ran down the stairs, dodging people trying to make it to the meeting upstairs, nearly tumbling down the steps with my hoop skirt knocking the unsuspecting out of my way. At the bottom, I mingled with the crowds to hide from Robert. I hunkered low in the mass of people knowing that a few would question their eyesight or maybe their sanity when I suddenly disappeared.

And then I was gone.

FOUR

WOOZY, I GRABBED AT the blouse stand, the shadows of two sales clerks lurking overhead. Lucinda reached under my arms and lifted me up. Then I remembered Nate and Jessica, and spun a little to check if they were still there. Still watching. Yup. Jessica was laughing. Laughing! Nate's eyebrows arched. With concern? I couldn't avoid peering into the rectangular mirror across the aisle. I was wearing the jeans and T-shirt I'd left in. The dark circles around my eyes were in full glory, as if I'd lost a boxing match.

"Let's go," Lucinda said gently. Agreeing to be my friend took heroics on some days. When I got home I crawled into bed. I managed to wiggle out of my clothes and into my PJs and snuggled under my quilt, falling into a heavy sleep.

The next morning I spent extra luscious moments lounging in the warmth and coziness of my bed. My experience gallivanting around Boston with Sara Watson in an impractical hoop skirt felt like a dream. It always did. I tried to relate to my travels like a dream life. This was my real life, my reality. This was where I had to try to build a life for myself. It wasn't easy.

"Casey!" My mom called me from the bottom of the stairs. "Your dad is here."

Oh. I'd forgotten about that. I rolled myself out of bed, and threw on clean jeans and a sweater. I made a quick pit stop in the bathroom, splashed water on my face and brushed my teeth. I passed Tim on the way down the steps.

"Dad's here," I said, in case he hadn't heard Mom bellow.

"Tell him I'm not coming." Tim was going through a punk phase, dressed all in black; his eyes looked suspiciously like he'd used "guy liner."

"Tim, you have to come. You missed last time." I followed him back upstairs. "Come, on Tim, you're not being fair."

Tim tilted his head and flashed a fake sympathetic smile. "Like Dad says, life's not fair."

"He misses you."

Tim stopped at his bedroom door. "Well, I don't miss him."

Great. I guess I was on my own again.

We lived in the outskirts of Cambridge in a white colonial house that had eight symmetrical windows of equal size each framed with black shutters. Our yard was sizable, with a fenced lawn, mature trees and large azaleas. Dad sat in a wicker chair on the back porch.

"Hey, Dad," I said, opening the screen door.

"Hi, Casey." He rose to give me a hug. "How's it going?"

"Pretty good." I shoved my hands in my pockets and rocked on my feet. Visitations always started off so awkwardly, like we were meeting each other for the first time. Not like when he'd lived with us and it'd been just normal to have him around. Didn't have to say 'hi, how are you?' all the time. We just knew.

"Where's Tim?"

"I don't know," I said, fudging.

"Isn't he coming?"

I could see Dad's disappointment. I hated to be the one to break the news. "I don't think so. Sorry."

"Oh. All right then. I guess it's just you and me."

I got into the passenger seat of his Passat as Dad folded his long body into the driver's side. My height and hair were from Dad, though his was cut so short you couldn't tell it was curly. Dad's skin was quite a bit darker than mine and Tim's, but because he was adopted, we didn't know what ethnicity was thrown into the mix. He reversed out of our driveway and headed in the direction of Boston.

"He's still mad, isn't he?" Dad finally stated.

Yes, Tim was still mad. My father's indiscretion with a co-worker was the reason Dad no longer lived with us.

"Timothy's mad at the world," I said, gawking at the blur of traffic. I pushed the images of horse drawn carriages out of my mind. "He'll come around."

"I hope so." He shifted into fourth and cleared his throat. "Does she talk about me?"

Uh-oh. Entering the uncomfortable zone. "She's not much of a talker," I said.

"Just so you know, I'm not proud of what I did."

Oh please. Do we have to talk about this? Normally, I like hanging with my dad, but this was awkward. I stared hard out the side window.

"If I could erase the past and start over," he continued, "I'd do it differently. Wouldn't it be great if we could just turn a switch and go back in time?"

Could life be more ironic? "I'm sure going to the past has its own sets of problems."

"I know, I know."

Uh, no, he didn't.

"Time travel is a myth," he ran his non-shifting hand through his almost non-existent hair, "but it's a nice fantasy."

If that's what you want to believe, Dad.

He sped up to pass a semi. "I want to come home, Casey."

Huh? "What do you mean?" Dad had rented a great brownstone townhouse in Back Bay when he moved out six months ago. It was close to the office building he worked in.

"I mean, I want to get back together with your mom."

Now I saw where this was all going. This was awesome! "Does she know that?"

"No. I haven't had the courage to tell her."

"Well, you need to tell her."

"She's not really talking to me right now."

"Tell her anyway." I felt bad for him; he looked so defeated. "Find a way. Send her flowers, write a love letter." Do something.

"Well, we'll see. Anyway, enough about me. How are you?"

"Fine."

"You have a boyfriend?"

What? Where'd that come from? "No!"

"That's a pretty strong 'no'. Are you sure?"

"Yes, I'm sure." As icky as it was, I much preferred talking about him and his problems. "There's nothing exciting going on in my life." Well, not from the usual time travel treks. "No secret romances." Unfortunately.

By the time we pulled into the underground parking at Copley Place, I'd had enough talking. There was a good cheesecake place there, and I planned on stuffing myself.

FIVE

I FOUGHT WITH MY HAIR, trying to "up-do" it with Bobby pins without much success. Mom knocked on my door just before I pulled my hair out of my head in frustration.

"Stupid hair. I don't know why I bother. It's not like I'm staying long. Don't be surprised to get a call from me soon after I get there."

"Oh, Casey. It's just a dance. Who knows, you might surprise yourself by having fun."

Uh, I didn't think so.

"Why couldn't I have gotten my hair from you?" I pouted. Mom had short, straight, shiny hair.

"You've got beautiful hair, Casey. You just have to know how to work it to your advantage."

"I don't possess hair skills." I threw the brush on the bed.

Mom promptly picked it up. "Can I have a shot?"

I sat on the edge of the bed. "Sure, Mom, work your magic."

My hair had grown over the last few weeks, and Mom managed to pin it up expertly and in moments. Not too tight, slightly messy, quaint curls falling around my face. Not bad.

"Wow, Mom. You're a lifesaver."

Next on the agenda: eyebrows.

She sat on my bed, watching as I attacked my face with a pair of tweezers. I had to hunch over, pressing close to the mirror to identify all the offending hairs.

"Why, if I had to get my hair from Dad, did I have to get his eyebrows, too?" I huffed. "Ouch."

"You don't have your dad's eyebrows, and there's nothing wrong with yours, Casey."

"They're huge!" Mom chuckled. "No, they're not. They're lovely and they suit you. They look like feathers."

I know she was trying to help, but really. Feathers? Enough pain; I put the tweezers down, then applied a bit of eye shadow (violet to go with my hazel eyes), mascara (brown to go with my hair), blush (to make my skin look rosy) and lip-gloss (so I could pretend there was a chance I might kiss a boy. Ha!).

I wasn't used to my look with make-up and I hoped I didn't come off like a clown. Mom helped me with the zipper at the back of my dress. "You look lovely, Casey."

"You think so?" I slipped on my only pair of dressy sandals, and frowned. "I'm not too tall, am I?"

"No. You look like a model. Every guy is going to want to dance with you, no matter how tall or short he is." Mothers can be so delusional.

Mom drove me to the high school gym where Lucinda waited for me near the door. Balancing carefully on my high heels I went to her.

"You look awesome," I said.

"You do too, Casey."

The gym was dark and it took a few moments for my eyes to adjust. A large mirrored globe slowly spun from the ceiling in the middle of the room, little sparkles of light flashing on the empty floor. Everyone was lined up along the wall, in cliques. The brains along one side, the artsies in the corner, the beauty queens near the punch bowl so everyone would have to look at how pretty they were when they got a drink, and the jocks tucked in just behind them, ogling as expected. Mr. Turner split up a grind in front of the stage.

I groaned. "Why did we come here, again?"

"It's going to be okay," said Lucinda. "There's a spot over there." She pointed to a space of bare wall across the gym from the brains, a little too close to the jocks.

"Beside the jocks?" I said. "Are you crazy?" Didn't she know who would be there? Of course she did. That's why she wanted us stationed there.

"It's where we'll get the best view. Hear the best stuff." She gave me a gentle shove and started walking. "We are fact finding, remember?" How could I forget when I felt like we were Dumb and Dumber, traipsing inelegantly across the gym floor, all eyes on us?

"Lucinda!" I hissed.

"Shh, the painful part is almost over."

Promises, promises. So, the loners—that would be us—stood alone behind the jocks, observing as they primped before the beauty queens who unabashedly flirted back. It was going to be a long night, and there was no way I was ever going to the refreshment table.

Nate stood in the midst of the jock group, along with his buds, Tyson, Dylan and Josh. They all looked amazing. And Nate, in a dark suit with a crisp white shirt and blue tie was—ah—stop it! I had to keep slapping myself so I wouldn't keep forgetting that I Hate Nate. The task got easier when I spotted Jessica, not, thankfully, in that white dress she'd had on at Filenes, but in a plainer, green number. So what if the color was fantastic with her strawberry blond hair?

Somehow, her evil radar picked it up— me trying not to stare.

She saw me and Lucinda standing against the brick wall like so much graffiti. I felt like an imbecile and cursed myself for having agreed to come. Forget THE Prom. I had all the facts I needed; I wouldn't be going to that. Actually, this was one fact I was glad to have gathered. Dances suck. Don't go.

Finally, the disk jockey got things going and called everyone to the floor. He had moderate success with all the couples leading the way, including smug Jessica with Nate. Watching them dance was pure torture. So she was pretty. So she was dancing with Nate. Why did I care? I forced myself to look at the glass globe spinning on the ceiling and stopped when I started feeling sick.

"When can we go, Luce?"

The song ended and Nate and Jessica returned to taunt me. "We just got here."

"That's not true. We've been here at least fifteen minutes. What else do we need to learn?" Besides alienation, rejection, humiliation? I tried to imagine what we looked like, standing against the wall barely changing position, wallflowers to the extreme. Maybe I should go get a chair. The disk jockey played song after song and the two of us remained by the wall as I had fully anticipated. Not that I wanted to dance. This wasn't *Dancing with the Stars*, people, just a bunch of geeky teens trying to keep a beat while getting away with sometimes questionable touching of persons of the opposite sex.

Jessica returned to the dance floor, this time with Craig the sophomore. He was okay looking, but I wondered why she kept teasing him. Besides the fact that Jessica Fuller would never date someone younger than she was (so I've heard), she had Nate. And why didn't Nate seem to care? Or did he? Maybe they were into open relationships? My legs were stiffening up. I checked my watch. One hour almost up. I was about to suggest a speedy departure when I felt a nudge in my side.

"It's Nate," Lucinda whispered. I know, Nate, Nate, Nate. She nudged me again. I looked to my right. I felt like a girl dying of thirst in the desert, convinced there was a stream of water running toward her. It really looked like Nate was walking our way.

I glanced behind me. Just a wall. Back to Nate. Yup, he was still walking towards us. My eyes popped wide. My brain was shutting down. I tried to remember my mantra. Hate Nate. Hate Nate. He stopped right in front of me. The only thing I could think of was how tall he was. Even with my heels on, he had to look down at me.

"Would you like to dance?" he said. To me. Nate to Casey. Wants to dance. I should have said no. My mind understood this. My spirit understood this. Somehow my mouth got it wrong and I heard myself say, "Okay."

The thing was it was a slow dance. He took my hand in his and put his other hand around my waist. I wasn't breathing. I put my free arm on his shoulder and gulped. Maybe I'd fainted from lack of punch and standing against the wall for too long, and this was just a hallucination.

He sure seemed real. He smelled good, spicy. Was I moving my feet? I was still standing so I must be breathing. My heart beat wildly. I was going to hyperventilate. When I dared to look at his face, he smiled. I was so confused! I stole a glimpse at the crowd by the punch table. Nate's friends were laughing. Jessica looked really mad, and pulled Craig tighter, if that were possible.

I was starting to enjoy this. We didn't talk, just swayed to the music. I wondered what life was going to be like for me post-dance. I would be miserable. Purely miserable, since Nate would surely never set eyes on me again. Jessica would make certain of that. I decided to just enjoy it for what it was.

"You look very nice tonight."

What? He spoke! He thought I looked nice. I was hyperventilating. I felt faint, dizzy. Was that bad? Nate was so strong, he would hold me up. Uh-oh, it was bad. Very, very bad. I wasn't dizzy because of Nate. Oh, no!

SIX

I GAPED AT NATE, AGHAST. I spun around and called out to heaven, "You've got to be kidding! As if things aren't bad enough, you have to let him come along?"I paced in small circles, trampling the grass, which was very uncharacteristic of me when I returned. I was usually poised, on my toes, ready for anything.

"What just happened?" Nate said, still calm. Sure he was calm now, but just wait. "Is this some kind of practical joke?"

I stopped pacing when my pointy heels sunk into a mossy part of the forest floor and faced him. I could see the wheels behind his eyes working; he was trying to figure out how his buddies had gotten him to the middle of the woods without him realizing it. Also, probably, why it was suddenly mid afternoon.

"Um, no," I squeaked out, still trying to process that I was back in 1860, and Nate Mackenzie was there right in front of me!

"Okay, guys, come out now." His eyes darted from tree to tree. I could see the panic forming. "Did they put something in my punch?" His voice took on that high edge that accompanies confusion.

"Oh, no," I moaned. My dress. I was wearing a totally inappropriate dress. And high heels! Could this day get any worse?

"What's the matter?"

"Nothing, it's my shoes." I took off one shoe and slammed the heel on a nearby boulder.

"Casey! What are you doing?"

"I'm, (bang) knocking (bang) off (bang) my heels." Success. I started with the next one.

"Why?"

"Because," I said in a voice suggesting he should know, though I knew there's no way he could know, "these are totally inappropriate for what we need to do next." This was exactly why I never wear heels. I was going to kill Lucinda when I got back.

Just then, I heard the faint clop of hooves and the din of voices. I grabbed Nate's hand and pulled him to the ground out of sight. Wow, Nate's hand was in my hand. A surge of electricity shot through my body. Mercifully, he pulled his hand away.

"What's going on? Casey, this isn't funny anymore."

"Shh." I put my finger to my lips. He cocked his head, hearing the voices now. Two men with top hats and cloaks with coat tails rode casually on the trail by our hiding spot. One of them said, "Abraham Lincoln will be the next president, mark my words, and then there will be hell to pay in the south."

"Role players?" said Nate. I gave him a stern look and returned my finger to my lips. When the riders were out of sight, I got up and motioned for Nate to follow me. I'd had time to get my bearings and I knew how to find my stash. It would take a long time to get there, especially in my heel-less, slippery, totally inappropriate shoes.

"Casey, what's happening? How did we get here?"

I pushed low branches out of the way and let out a long breath. "Okay. It's just I don't think you're going to believe it."

"Try me."

I was glad I couldn't see his face. "We've gone back in time."

"Whoa. Say again? I don't think I heard you correctly."

I stopped and turned to him. He slanted his head and bent toward me slightly, not wanting to miss what I had to say. His eyes were imploring, and his face ruggedly handsome...

"Casey!"

"Oh, sorry. Um, I said, we went back in time."

"We went back in time. Really?" He stood up straight. The muscles in his jaw tightened. He didn't believe me. Fine, don't believe me. Make this day suck even more. I turned around and kept walking. He followed. Nate didn't like the silence, or maybe he just didn't like not being in control. I pulled the pins out of my up-do and let it fall down my back.

"Okay, Casey, say I believe you. But why should I? There could be a perfectly good explanation for this."

"It's mid afternoon," I said.

"I see that."

"So, just a short while ago," I paused and remembered, we were dancing, "it was dark. Night-time."

"Okay, so as a joke they drugged me, and it lasted several hours."

"Not a very funny joke."

He ignored me, "I woke up in the middle of the woods, somewhere in Massachusetts. We're still in Massachusetts aren't we?" I nodded. "The guys didn't feel like waiting for me to wake up."

"The guys?" I said.

"Yeah, Tyson and Josh. I should have known they were up to no good when they dar..."

I stopped and swiveled around on one slippery shoe. "They dared you? That's why you asked me to dance? A dare?"

The truth registered with my head and made a knife cut right into my heart. I Hate Nate. I spun back around and plowed my way through the bushes.

"No, Casey, I meant..."

"Oh, just drop it."

We rounded a corner and I saw the lilac grove. I sighed. Home Sweet Home away from home. I pushed through the bramble into the center, Nate on my heels.

"If you don't believe me," I said, "then why are you following me?"

"I don't know. You look like you know where you're going."

"I do." I dragged off the twig thatch and revealed the hole. I pulled out the goods, enjoying the stunned look on Nate's face.

"If this was a practical joke," Nate said, "then you'd have to be in on it."

"How realistic is that?"

"Not very," Nate admitted.

I took a swig from the water jar. Ick, even worse tasting than before, but it was wet. I offered it to Nate.

"Ew." He spit out the water.

"Hey, don't waste that. You don't know when we will be able to get more."

"Fine, I'll play along. What's next in the game?"

I sat down on the log, stretched my legs out and threw off my stupid shoes. My feet ached. I supposed curling up and having a nap was not on the agenda. Nate sat on the grass across from me.

"So, any food? Did the guys at least pack me a lunch?"

I threw the burlap bag with the dried beef at him. "Help yourself."It wasn't the same as the stuff you buy at the convenience store, but it seemed to hit the spot. He didn't complain. I lay down, putting my hands behind my head and closed my eyes. I needed to think. Think, think, think. I was here with Nate. Maybe this would be a really short trip, and before I knew it, we'd be back, and he could beat up his friends for pulling a stupid practical joke and leaving him alone in the woods with me, the gullible loser.

We'd have to stay close because to get him back I'd have to be touching him, skin to skin. If I wasn't so freaked out, I'd be happy about that idea. I waited. Nothing. Nate took his cue from me and lay down, too. I guessed he'd resigned himself to just waiting it out, for his guys to get bored of the joke and pop out of the trees.

The sun started its trek downward. My stomach growled. I pulled the burlap bag to my side and looked in it. All the beef was gone.

"You ate it all?"

"Wasn't I supposed to?"

"No!"

"Hey, chill out. This can't last much longer."

Oh yes it could. It could last much, much longer. We were out of dried beef, but still had a few raisins, which I munched on. We were almost out of drinking water. The sun was a quarter way down. It would be dark in a couple hours.

My stomach growled again and I knew it was time for action. I took the hatchet and dug a small hole. I scoped the bushes for dry branches, leaves, dead moss, anything that would burn and placed them in the hole. The whole time I was aware of Nate watching my every move. He didn't understand survival the way I did. And I didn't care if I was parading around in bare feet and a *saffron* dress!

With the edge of the hatchet and the flint, I created a spark. Blowing softly, I managed to get the dead moss lighted. Soon the whole thing was aflame, and I added bigger twigs and branches to keep it going.

"You're a Girl Scout?"

I ignored him. When the fire was burning on its own, I picked up the slingshot. I found a small stone and waited. After a few moments a quail scurried across the far end of the grove. I took careful aim and shot. Bingo.

"Wow!" said Nate. I'd momentarily forgotten he was there. He watched me use the hatchet to chop the head off, pluck the feathers and again with the hatchet, slice a line down the stomach and dump the guts out. Wasps came out of nowhere, and I shooed them away with my hands.

"They love the smell of blood," I explained.

"All the girls I know would be freaking right now," Nate said, admiration evident on his face. A first. I threw all the innards but the gizzard and heart into the fire, which responded with loud hissing. Then I chiseled a sharp point at the end of a stick, which I used to impale the little carcass along with its organs. Couldn't afford to waste any chance at protein. I held the bird over the fire to cook it.

"Where'd you learn to do all this stuff?" said Nate. More admiration. *That's right, pile it on.*

"Here, in the past." It was amazing what hunger and the drive to survive could give you the will to do. I admitted it took quite a few tries before my hunting chops were up.

"Oh, right. Time travel."

I ignored his sarcasm, and spun my stick. The meat was giving off a strong, mouth-watering aroma.

"Kind of like a big marshmallow roast," said Nate. "Good idea."

"Thanks." I decided to tease him. "Where's yours? You don't expect me to share, do you?"

He seemed startled by that. "Um, well..."

I pointed to the slingshot. "Go for it."

He walked over and gingerly picked it off the ground. He examined its crudeness. "You didn't pick this up at Wal-Mart, did you?"

Uh, no. He found a small stone, crouched low, mimicking my

earlier performance, and waited. A quail sprinted across and he shot. Miss.

"I'm rusty."

"Rusty implies that you have previous experience," I said smugly.

"Okay, I suck. Is that better?"

"Marginally." I licked my fingers and, after his third miss, I had pity.

"Now that you can feel the speed at which the stone moves, aim a fraction in front of the bird. They're fast."

Nate threw me a look, which I couldn't read. Gratitude or annoyance? However, it worked. He hit it.

"Yes! Dinner."

I refused to help him with the plucking and gutting, but enjoyed watching him struggle. I had to admit he did pretty well for his first effort. His bird was roasting nicely, and he seemed very pleased with himself.

"Good job," I said.

"Thanks."

Dusk glowed with an orange hue. After throwing more branches onto the fire, I took the clothes from the burlap bag and created a makeshift bed for myself, lying on the bag, using the ivory dress with the little bluebells stitched on it as a blanket. Nate watched with great interest.

"You look serious."

"What do you mean?"

"You look like you intend to stay here the night."

"It's a good possibility."

He lay down on the grass opposite me, the small fire a careful boundary.

"Well, at least it's a beautiful night. Look at all those stars. I don't remember a night so bright with stars like this."

"That's because there's no light pollution."

"Right." He rubbed the very sexy stubble growing on his chin. "So, say I go along with your story," Nate said. "Where are we?"

"Just outside of Cambridge."

"And, uh, when are we?"

"It's 1860."

"How do you know?"

"Because that's when it was the last time I was here."

"Which was?"

"A couple weeks ago."

"A couple weeks?"

"That's what I said."

"Uh huh. Okay. So what's happening in America in 1860?"

I thought of Sara Watson and Robert Willingsworth. "Abolition is a big issue. It's hard for many to imagine a functioning economy without slave labor. The women wear these humongous hoop slips under their dresses, totally inefficient, just another example of fashion restricting women in the name of beauty. And, of course, Abraham Lincoln gets elected president on November sixth."

Nate chuckled. "You know your history."

I shrugged. "Wouldn't you, if you were me?"

"Anyway, it's been fun and all that. Haven't been punk'd like this before, but time's up," Nate said. "Let's go."

Time's up? He had no clue. "Go where?" Couldn't he see we were in the middle of nowhere?

"Back to the dance, home, wherever. We're not really going to spend the night out here are we?"

I let out a frustrated breath. "Well, if you want to go, feel free." The moonlight reflected his perfect face, the newly forming shadow of facial hair and his deep set intelligent eyes. He made a point of looking every direction, the reality of our situation seeping in. I rolled over, my back to him; otherwise, I might never get to sleep. I couldn't believe I was spending the night with Nate Mackenzie (sort of).

We woke up early and finished off the water. Nate didn't spit it out this time.

"No guys?" I couldn't help but say.

"No. I'm going to pummel them when they show."

We were out of food and water. We had no choice but to head out. I picked up the dress I'd used as a blanket and tried to shake out the wrinkles. I hid behind one of the bushes, but it wasn't exactly a changing room.

"Turn around," I said. Nate was confused, but did it. I struggled with the zipper at the back of my dance dress and managed to pull it down. That's one good thing about having long limbs. I slipped out of the dress, and pulled the ivory one over my head. It was tight.

And short.

"Oh, no," I gasped.

"What?" said Nate, turning.

"Don't look!"

"Oh, sorry. What are you doing?"

"I'm changing my dress. I can't go out there looking like that."

"Looking like what?"

"Like I just came off a dance floor in the 21st century."

The ivory dress was too short. Why couldn't I just stop growing! I tugged harder, attempting to do up the buttons at my chest, but it was too tight. Then it dawned on me. I'd grown! I was giddy. Finally I had grown in the area I'd wanted to grow. But still, I had a problem with the dress not fitting. I slipped back into my yellow dance dress. Nate's suit was a bit ruffled from his night sleeping on the ground, but he still looked great, and my heart stubbornly fluttered.

"Let's go find a bus," he said.

"A bus? You still don't get it, do you?"

"Oh, right. We're back in time."

I covered my face with my hands. What a mess! It was bad enough when I had to scout and sneak for my own survival, but now I had HIM, an unbeliever. We were out of food and water, dressed in a way that would get us thrown into jail. Well, me anyway. Not to mention how unacceptable it was in 1860 for a girl my age to be accompanied by a boy his age without a chaperone.

"Casey? Are you okay?

No! I'm not. "I'm fine. Look, here's what we'll do. I know of a place near here where we can get some clothes."

Not the Watson farm. I didn't like to steal from them.

"Yeah, I wouldn't mind getting into some jeans, watch a game on my flat screen."

"We'll have to pretend that you're my brother."

"Huh?"

I could tell that the only way he was going to believe me was if he saw it for himself.

"Let's go."

SEVEN

"REMIND ME AGAIN, why I'm following you?"

I let a sizable branch whip behind me, feeling a certain amount of satisfaction when it smacked Nate in the face.

"Hey!"

"Because I know where I'm going."

"Is that why we're hacking through brush alongside the road instead of walking on the road?"

We're hacking through brush because you asked me to dance on a dare. "Yup."

My dress didn't provide much warmth for mid October, but my nervous energy kept me warm enough. The musty, damp smell of compost under our shoes wafted up as we trekked through the carpet of yellow and red leaves. I grabbed bare branches to keep from slipping; my shoes lacked traction and felt more like skates. The spotty foliage worked against concealing our presence.

"Okay, you win." Nate stopped, throwing his hands in the air. "It was a funny joke, but, you know, it's getting old."

At that moment a carriage trotted around the corner towards us. Unlike Willie's cart and goat, this carriage looked like it came straight out of Cinderella. The driver wore a suit with tails, and I glimpsed a wide brimmed fancy hat through one of the windows. I squatted down, pulling Nate with me. At least my yellow dress blended in.

"What was that?" he said after it passed out of view.

"Exactly what it looked like."

"Where are we, Casey?"

"Like I told you yesterday, we're just outside of Cambridge."

"Man, I'm messed up. I can't get my bearings."

We got to the edge of the Cummings' property. Smoke rose from the chimney of a two-story house set in from the road. I'd been here before and knew the Cummingses had lots of kids. Proof hung on the line out back, trousers of every size and several long linen dresses.

Unfortunately, the yard wasn't empty. Three young boys played ball with a puppy. I squatted low, motioning for Nate to do the same.

"We're going to have to wait it out."

"Wait what out? Why don't we just go ask to use the phone?" He took a step out of the underbrush.

"No!" I grabbed his arm and tugged him back so hard I stumbled, pulling him down on the ground with me.

"Hey!" He landed with a soft thump, pressed up against my side. Close. I could feel his chest move as he breathed. Our eyes locked and I shuddered internally, like someone had pulled a thread from the seam of my being. I wondered if he felt it, too.

"Sorry, Nate," I said softly, "but you can't do that."

Just then Mrs. Cummings walked out onto the deck and screeched like an army sergeant at her kids to come in for breakfast. She was a robust woman with an apron tied around a full, floor length gray skirt. She had that no-nonsense expression worn by some teachers I knew.

Nate leaned up on one elbow, analyzing the scene. The puppy followed the little boys into the house and an older girl, also in a long dress and apron, stepped out of a chicken coop with a basket of eggs. I supposed to Nate, she looked like she was still in her nightgown.

Mr. Cummings and the older boys had probably already eaten breakfast and were working at the textile mill. With the exception of a braying donkey, the yard was quiet. I had my window of opportunity.

"Wait here," I said. Nate seemed too stunned to argue. Despite my stupid shoes I moved stealthily through the brush, keeping low to the ground. My stomach grumbled, but I pushed thoughts of food aside. At the line I plucked a dress and a pair of trousers I hoped would fit Nate. I scurried away and thought I was home free until I heard the cocking of a gun.

"Come back with my laundry, you low life trash!"

A stout Mrs. Cummings stood on the porch with a rifle aimed in my direction. Nate's eyes were as wide as quarters. Mrs. Cummings wasn't messing around. A boom filled the air, a bullet splintering the tree to my left.

"Run!"

Nate and I sprinted into the denseness of the forest, two more shots whizzing over our heads. I lagged behind, my slippery shoes no help at all.

"Nate!" He reached back and grabbed my hand, dragging me as he darted wildly through brush, dodging branches, lobbing over fallen trees. Nate may have been a star athlete, but I sure wasn't. My lungs burned.

"I think. She stopped." I said, wheezing like an asthmatic. Nate stretched tall, listening. All quiet but for my rasping breath.

Once I knew we were out of firing range, and that no one was chasing us, I paid attention to the fact that Nate was still holding my hand.

Nate stared at me, utter disbelief on his face. "Casey? What the heck?"

He released my hand and I tossed him the trousers.

"Wow," I said. "I've never been shot at before."

"You're a freakin' thief," he said. I took a deep breath.

"I like to think of it as a loan."

"You're nuts, girl. Looney tunes."

Obviously he wasn't fazed at all by our recent hand holding experience. "I'd put those on if I were you," I said.

He shook his head. "I think I'm done playing around, Casey."

"Fine," I said with a grin. "But you split your pants."

He twisted around to look. A big rip ran down his left butt cheek to the back of his leg, revealing blue boxers. I think he actually blushed. I spotted a crevice in the side of the hill where I took my newly acquired article of clothing to change in privacy. The dress fit okay. A little short but just snug enough in the chest area. I still needed proper shoes and a hat, but I'd worry about that later.

When I went back for Nate, I couldn't find him. "Nate?" I scoured the area, but nothing.

"Nate? Where are you?" I tried to guess which way he'd gone. "Na-a-a-te!" This wasn't funny! What if I lost Nate? He couldn't get back without me. There'd be a massive manhunt when I got back. They would know it was me somehow. I'd go to jail. "Nate!" How'd he survive here in the past alone? He'd get into trouble for sure. He'd go to jail. My throat was closing up with nerves. I couldn't swallow. My forehead felt moist with perspiration. I had to find him. "Nate!"

"I'm over here," He came walking out of the trees, suit gone, trousers on, sleeves of his white shirt rolled up. Gorgeous.

"Don't do that to me!" I stammered.

"What? Were you afraid? Little Miss I Know How to Survive."

Please God, could we just go back now? I didn't know how much more of this I could take.

"I'm not afraid for me."

He was staring again.

"What?"

"That dress suits you."

"Shut up."

"Hey, it was a compliment. Don't bite my head off."

Did he really mean it? He thought I looked good? Nah. He was smirking.

"Just stick with me from now on, okay?"

"Yes, ma-am." He saluted. I stormed away. I Hate Nate. He caught up effortlessly. We detoured south until we hit a dirt road.

"What's next?" Nate said. "Food, I hope. The guys better have beer and wings waiting."

Dream on, buddy. "There should be a highway or something, somewhere."

"We're on a main road now," I said.

"I mean something paved."

"You could be waiting a while." I'd planned to keep going past the Watson Farm because I was unprepared to answer to Sara. Though I doubted that she had minded being left alone with Robert Willingsworth. But by the time we arrived my feet were dying and my stomach protested bitterly. Nate added his complaints without restraint.

"We've been walking for miles; we must be near a major roadway."

A vast lawn stretched toward the road from the front of the manor. A garden spread out behind it leading to the barn. In the distance, I could see the lake.

"Wow," said Nate. "They did a great job restoring this place."

"Actually, in our time, it's a shopping mall." Sara was in the garden along with a collection of younger Watsons.

"Jonathon and Michael, quit fooling around. If you want to eat this winter, you'll mind me and get to work." Mounds of potatoes and carrots dotted the soil and I nearly snatched one, dirt and all, to scarf it down.

"Cassandra?" she said when she spotted me. Her eyes reviewed my attire and windblown hair. "What happened to you?" I'd been thinking of an excuse for the last five miles.

"Sara, I'd like you to meet my brother, Nate, uh, Nathaniel." He squinted at me. If I had to be Cassandra, he could be Nathaniel.

"Like the author," she said. Seeing his confusion she added, "Hawthorne, Nathaniel Hawthorne. She reached out her hand. "I'm Sara. It's nice to meet you." Then back to me. "Cassandra? What happened to you? You told Robert you were faint and left Faneuil Hall before Abby Foster even started her lecture. We searched everywhere for you. I was worried."

Nate listened with narrowing eyes. Then he scoured the yard and the sky. "Where are the power lines?"

I noted Sara's confusion. "Sara, we've had a long day of travel, and my brother isn't feeling well..."

"Oh, excuse my manners. Come in for some tea and I'll fix you something to eat while you explain everything to me."

"Casey, I'm weirding out here."

"I already tried to explain," I said. Sara glanced over her shoulder at us. I lowered my voice. "Let me do the talking, okay."

"Is this a commune? Why does everyone dress like that?"

"Shh. Just keep your mouth shut."

We went through the back kitchen entrance and took a seat at the long wooden kitchen table. Though it was luxurious for

1860, I tried to see it through Nate's point of view. The wood burning stove and grill, the kind you find in museums, small icebox, pitcher and large bowl for water. Nate's eyes darted back and forth. I could sense him mentally trying to put together all the pieces.

Sara cooked up pancakes and scrambled eggs, enough for an army. Soon we were surrounded by a mass of noisy, dirty children and choruses of "Move over, You're in my spot, I was here first."

"Children!" Sara commanded. Amazingly, they fell immediately silent. "Josephine, please take a plate up to Mother." To us, "Missy comes in three days a week to help out. Today is her day off."

Willie walked in, dropped a newspaper on the counter, pulled the chair at the head of the table out and sat down. He blew stray red curly locks from his eyes. I kept my head down, letting my loose curls hide my face. Did Sara mention my deception? Does Willie know that I'm a girl? Fortunately, the other smaller Watsons distracted him from me for the time being.

Cobbs came in next, setting his big butt in the chair nearest the door. He didn't care about manners and openly stared at me. Creeper! Willie said grace and everyone dug in, Nate and I wolfing down our serving in record time. Sara leaned back with a scowl on her face.

"I'm sorry," I said. "Our manners are atrocious."

Cobbs finished quickly, offered a weak thank you and left.

Willie must have been famished too. He waited until his dish was empty to speak. "I'm afraid my manners are dismal as well. Sara, I haven't been introduced to our new friends."

Sara looked quickly at me. "This is Cassandra and her brother Nathaniel."

Willie studied me. Hard. So, Sara hadn't mentioned my lie. I could see his mind computing, unbelieving. "C-Casey?" The hurt in his voice was loud and clear. Nate could tell something was up, and stopped eating.

"You're a girl?"

"Willie, I pretended to be a boy, because it was easier for me to get work."

"But, we, uh, I..." I could tell he was trying to remember if he had taken any boy/hygiene liberties around me. He hadn't, I'd made sure of that, for myself as well.

Willie stood with a start. "Sara, you knew about this?"

"It's a recent discovery." His face flamed red as his hair.

"Willie," I said standing with him, "I didn't mean to deceive you."

He lifted the newspaper off the counter and slapped it onto the table. After a beat he left, letting the door slam behind him. Nate looked shell shocked by the whole exchange. He reached for the newspaper and scanned the front page. I read over his shoulder: The Boston Journal, October 11, 1860.

Nate's face paled. He didn't look well. "Are you okay?" I said.

"I thought you were joking," he said weakly. Ah, he was converting.

"You don't look like brother and sister," Sara said. Now what were we going to do? She'd caught us. Or so I thought. "Although, I don't look like half my siblings either." She walked to the door. "We have an empty workers' cabin out by the lake. I'll take you there."

My legs ached, and I barely had the strength to make it the hundred yards to the cabin. Nate followed in a zombie-like state. I hoped he wasn't going into shock. The cabin was a small, maybe twelve by twelve wooden structure. A narrow footpath through high grass wound around from the front door to the back, I assumed to the outhouse.

"You both look like you need a good night's sleep." Sara's said. "Cassandra, I'll expect you in the kitchen when the rooster crows tomorrow morning. Nathaniel, you can meet up with Willie in the barn." She walked inside and opened the lone window.

Now, quite honestly, I'd expected two rooms. Really. "We're sharing?" I squeaked, but she had already gone back to the demands of her busy home.

EIGHT

THE COTS CREAKED WHEN we sat on them. We faced each other across the small room like two combatants before the gun blows. And it was worse than that. Despite the grueling hike and the baggy trousers and the tense expression on his face, Nate was still adorable. How would I manage sharing a room with Nate? This was so awkward!

"Start talking," he said.

"What do you want me to say?"

His left eyebrow inched up.

"Okay. I told you from the beginning, I did some time traveling."

"Yeah, an unusual hobby."

"Do you want me to talk or what?"

I took it by his silence and dark shade of his blue-eyed stare that he did. "Sometimes, I travel, but," I lightened my voice, "I always go back."

"Back to when?"

"Right back to where I left. No one will even notice that you've been gone."

"That's good. Jessica would be so ticked if I took off without telling her."

I winced. Evil Jessica Fuller. I'd forgotten about her here. The one good thing about traveling is that I don't have to deal with her. Nate noticed I'd grown silent.

"You don't like her?"

"So what if I do or I don't?"

"No reason. Just wondering."

"She doesn't like me."

"Why wouldn't she like you?"

"She's your girlfriend. Ask her yourself. And really, since we're getting all cozy here, I have to ask, what do you see in her?"

He just shrugged.

"Whatever, I don't care." I didn't want to talk about her. I guess he didn't either.

"So, how do we get back?" He said this with a big sigh.

"Um, I don't know how that works exactly."

His jaw dropped. "You don't know how it works!"

"Not really, it just happens."

"Without warning?"

"Oh, no, I get a bit of lead time going back. It's coming here that I'm caught off guard. Otherwise, well, I'd be here alone."

That seemed to strike him.

"How often does this happen to you?"

"When I was younger, maybe once, twice a year, but recently, it's really picked up. Not sure why. I think it has something to do with stress."

Slow dancing with Nate Mackenzie. Walking in high heels across the gym floor under a strobe light. Being mocked by a particular pretty, if stuck up, red headed cheerleader. Slow dancing with Nate Mackenzie.

He flipped his legs onto his cot and lay down, hands under

his head. "This is so sci-fi. But kind of cool, when you think about it."

I'm glad he thought so. I examined our new home. Wooden floors, two cots with a night table between them—a candle and box of matches the only thing on it—and a larger table under the window with a pitcher and bowl for washing up. A small brick fireplace was built into the corner with a little pile of kindling and a stack of wood against the wall. I lit the candle, then stepped across the room, the wooden floor squeaking under my feet. I poured a bit of water into the bowl, scooped it up and splashed it on my face. I breathed in deeply. Somehow we'd make it through this.

I returned to my cot and let myself recline. My body ached and trembled with exhaustion. Nate turned on his side and faced me.

"How old were you the first time it happened?"

"Nine."

"That must have been scary for you."

"It was." I related my Jungle Book boy experience.

"How long does it last?"

"Sometimes it's as short as a few hours and sometimes..."

Like the summer I first met Willie...

"Sometimes..." Nate prodded.

"It's longer. I never know. Hopefully it'll just be a couple days."

"Does this happen to anyone else you know?"

"I haven't met anyone. I know the signs and I haven't seen the evidence."

"There are signs?"

"Well, a few. I get dark rings around my eyes when I travel back to my time; I'm discombobulated for a while, and really, really tired."

Nate took this in letting his eyelids close. "So, you're a time traveler. I'm not. How do I get back?"

"You have to be touching me. Skin to skin." His eyes were shut but he was smiling. If I'd had a spare pillow, I'd have chucked it at him. Instead I got off my cot and headed outside.

"Where you off to?"

"The outhouse."

"Hey, Casey?"

I stopped at the door. "Yeah?"

"What happens if, you know, you don't get to me on time, to touch my skin?"

"You'd get left here, I guess."

The muscles around his eyes tightened, making them bulge a little. I added quickly, "I'd come back eventually, so you wouldn't be left here forever."

"Awesome," he said sarcastically.

I really had to go, but felt worried now about leaving him alone. What if it did happen when we were apart? I'd go back to the dance, and Nate would be gone. To everyone else, he'd have just "poofed" into mid air. How would I explain that? It would be disastrous. I decided to make my trip to the outhouse a quick one.

When I returned, Nate headed out.

"Just follow the trail through the grass," I shouted after him. "Blow the candle out when you get back."

I watched his back as he left the cabin, still not believing I was here with Nate Mackenzie and that we were about to fall asleep in the same room. Oh, my goodness. Best not to think about it too much. Mercifully, I fell asleep quickly and didn't spring awake until the nerve-wracking crow of the rooster at dawn.

Two pair of boots sat outside our cabin door. If the Watson sibs were anything, they were observant. Willie showed up to take Nate on a tour of the farm. I pulled him aside before they left. "Willie, I don't blame you for being mad."

"I confess that I was hurt Casey, uh, Cassandra. A man doesn't like to be played the fool. But after I thought about it for a while, I saw that you only did it as a protection for yourself. I don't know why your father or brothers let you go off on your own, and it's not my place to judge. But I understand it would have been foolhardy for you to travel alone as a girl. Uh, woman."

"So, we're still friends?" I asked hopefully.

He smiled. "Friends."

We did the awkward should-we-shake-hands-or-hug dance (I, for one, avoid shaking bare hands when possible), then I grabbed him and gave him a quick, platonic hug. I headed to the house to help with breakfast. My first task was to go back outside and get a pail of water from the pump. With no tap to turn, I had to physically pump the handle as water poured out of a spigot into the bucket.

Back in the kitchen, I used the water to make a big pot of porridge. While I was getting water, a guest had arrived. Sara introduced him to me as Samuel Jones. He looked to be in his late teens and had the same wild-eyed hungry look that Nate and I had arrived with. And he was black. Not a big deal in a world where the president is African American, but an issue during 1860 with the civil war looming.

Nate, Willie and Cobbs showed up shortly after and Sara made the introductions again. Cobbs grunted and sat down.

"Hey," Nate said to Samuel. "How's it going?"

"Good now," Samuel said. "It smells like heaven in here."

Sara called the children and put the pot of porridge on the table. We all helped ourselves to generous portions.

"So, Sam," Nate said, "you here long? I'd offer you to bunk with me, but my sister," he grinned at me, "is taking up all the space."

He spoke to Samuel with the same familiarity he did with his friend Tyson. I didn't know if he noticed the stunned looks of our hosts and of Samuel himself. White folks here just didn't talk like that to those who weren't white. I turned to Nate and gave him my best "zip it!" glare.

"That's fine," Samuel said softly. "I won't be here for long."

"Samuel has recently come from the south," Sara offered.

Ah, a runaway slave, perhaps? He had a likable face, strong yet vulnerable. I felt worried for him.

"He should be safe here," I ventured. "With Massachusetts being a free state."

There was a pregnant pause. Did I just say something I shouldn't have?

"That's true," Willie responded, "But don't forget about the fugitive act."

Right. Stupid me, I knew that.

"I'm waiting for my younger brother Jonah," Samuel said. "Then we'll head up to Canada."

"Oh," said Nate. "I'm from Canada."

Why, oh why couldn't he just keep his mouth shut?

"Really?" said Willie.

"I thought you were from Springfield."

"We are," I jumped in, "Nathaniel meant our grandfather on our mother's side originally came from Canada. We've never been there."

I picked up the brown sugar. "Sugar, anyone?" Sara poured the coffee and we managed to keep the conversation tame. Samuel and Nate left for the barn and I did the dishes. It took forever. Again I had to pump water from outside and haul it in, then heat the water on the stove before filling the sink.

When I finally had the last bowl washed, dried and put away Sara called for me. "Mother's feeling better today and would like to pass the time in the sitting room. I require your assistance to help her down the stairs."

"Sure." The last time I had seen Mrs. Watson, which had been some time ago now, she'd been commanding the kitchen, fully in the role that Sara played. Now she was petite and wiry, like a broomstick in a skirt. Despite her bulging stomach, Mrs. Watson was still a waif of a woman. Her dark hair was salted with gray and pulled into a bun at the back of her head. She had pouchy skin with deep lines on her forehead and brow. She looked too old to be having children to me, but what did I know?

The sitting room was warmly decorated with a wall of shelves filled with books and a colorful area rug dotted with a selection of high back chairs. Sara and I settled her into one nearest the massive stone fireplace. The fire burned gently with sporadic sparks; the room felt like a Christmas card.

"Thank you Sara and..."

"It's Cassandra, Mother," Sara said. "She's the new girl I told you about."

"Yes, well, thank you Cassandra, for helping my dear Sara. I honestly don't know what I'd do without her."

"Well, we won't worry about that today." Sara draped a shawl around her mother's shoulders.

"I bet you'll be glad once Mr. Watson returns," I said.

"Oh, he won't be back in time to see this little one come into the world," Mrs. Watson said. "It takes many weeks to travel to London and back."

Mr. Watson didn't plan to be here for the birth of his own kid? I guess number ten wasn't much to celebrate.

Afterwards, I helped Sara can vegetables for the winter. Then I made supper. And did the dishes again. At least the younger girls helped with that, though sometimes they didn't feel very helpful.

Before returning to the cabin, I found a ball of string and an extra bed sheet. An idea had been bouncing around my mind all day, and I immediately put it into action. I strung a line of string from the front wall of the cabin to the back and clothes-pinned the sheet to it, separating the room. I wasn't Nate's sister and I had no plans of letting him view what wasn't his.

And so went our first day. Then our second. On our third I grabbed Nate and made a surreptitious trip to the grove to restock the stash. With proper boots we were only MIA from the farm for an hour. Nate got that I needed to prepare for my next trip back and even a long walk was still a break from working. By the fourth day my back burned and I'd have died for a hot bath. Nate walked around like an old man. No matter that he was a super fit athlete; it didn't prepare you for the rigors of mind numbing, backbreaking labor. Nate walked in at the end of the day, just as I lit the candle, and flopped on his cot.

"I thought you said a couple days," he mumbled.

"Well," I said from the privacy of my side of the sheet. "Usually it is. I'm sure I'll be shouting your name soon."

I'd promised him I'd come running to the barn calling his name when I felt the "trip" start.

"You better get ready," I said, removing my work dress. "We're supposed to meet Robert Willingsworth in Boston. Finally, we get to do something interesting."

"You know, I can see your silhouette with the candle burning."

"What!" I grabbed the "going to town" dress Sara had lent me and covered myself. "Close your eyes!" I heard him chuckle. "Shut up!" I really wanted to throw something at him. I'd been very careful when selecting the sheet making sure there weren't any holes. No peek-a-booing going to happen here. I didn't account for silhouetting, though.

"Be a gentleman and turn around."

"And if I don't?" his voice had that annoying little lilt I used to find amusing.

"If you don't, I'll—I'll tell Jessica!" Teasing me, he said, "Jessica who?"

"Your girlfriend."

"Oh, her. No need to freak. I've been turned around for ten minutes already."

Humph. I slipped into the dress, thankful that the buttons ran up the front, and then pulled on the socially required but ridiculous hoop skirt underneath. I'd get Sara to help me with my hair, I thought, as I marched out of the cabin, covering my ears to block out Nate's laughter.

We took one of two carriages owned by the Watsons.

"We need to use both," Sara explained, "to get the whole Watson family to church on Sundays."

Nate gawked out the window. I had to elbow him and whisper, "close your mouth." I remembered seeing it for the first time: Boston with no automobiles or electric streetlights, movie-set-like costumes, lots of horses and black or Irish men pushing wheelbarrows and shoveling manure. All the modern buildings and glass and steel skyscrapers, like The John Hancock Tower, that are cramped beside the old brick buildings on the Freedom Trail, gone.

The doors of an Irish pub opened up as we clip-clopped by. Cobbs stumbled out just in time to see me staring out the coach window. He offered a smarmy grin and saluted.

"I don't like that guy," Nate whispered.

"I guess he didn't want to join us tonight."

It had grown dark by the time we reached our destination. The oil lamps lighting the streets dimly illuminated the sign on the building: The United States Hotel. Nate surprised me by offering his hand to assist me out of the carriage. He wore a borrowed unbuttoned waistcoat over his own white dress shirt, suspenders, boots and a topcoat. I almost didn't hate him in that moment.

The United States Hotel was an elaborate brick structure bound by Beach, Lincoln and Kingston Streets, and in 1860 was the largest in the country. It stood three stories high and took up three whole blocks. Sara and Willie greeted the doorman.

"This isn't around anymore?" Nate stated the obvious.

I shook my head, "Now we have Chinatown."

The cobble roads were a bustle of activity. Other carriages passed by or stopped in front of the hotel. Solo riders on horseback clip-clopped alongside a mass of pedestrians. Across the street a band of black men stood quietly, holding a banner with a hand painted slogan that said, ABOLISH THE FUGITIVE ACT.

I spotted Samuel Jones. He acknowledged me with a slight nod. The gentlemanly doorman opened the double doors and a porter directed us to a large meeting room. It was a political gathering, with the keynote speaker due to discuss the hot issues of states' rights and slavery.

Nate spoke softly in my ear, "Will we see Lincoln?"

"No, but if you look to your right you'll see Ralph Waldo Emerson seated beside Nathaniel Hawthorne."

"Ah, the author," he added, mimicking Sara.

Sara had spotted Robert Willingsworth and gone to him. The sparkle in her eye said it all—she was in love. Unfortunately, Robert was looking over her head. At me. Decorum demanded that he converse with her, but after politely asking about her family and her health, he marched in my direction.

"Miss Donovan!" He grabbed my hand— thankfully Sara had lent me a pair of white gloves— and graciously kissed it. "What in heaven's name happened to you at Faneuil Hall? You disappeared into thin air!"

Nate's eyes flashed with amusement, and he bit his lip to keep from laughing. I wanted to kick him in the shin.

"Yes, I had to leave suddenly. A courier had delivered news that my mother was very ill and I rushed home immediately."

"I'm so sorry to hear that."

Sara, having trailed behind Robert, her sparkle and spunk gone, added, "But, she returned to us with her brother."

"Oh, yes." I broached an awkward introduction. "Robert, I'd like you to meet my, uh, brother, Nathaniel."

"Mr. Donovan," Robert said, stretching out his hand, "it's my pleasure."

Mr. Donovan? Now it was my turn to bite my lip. We selected a table and played a little game of musical chairs. It seemed Robert fully intended to sit next to me, a performance I found irritating. Nate sat on my other side.

"He is so into you," Nate whispered. His eyes widened when he said this. Was he surprised that I could attract a man's attention?

"Shh!"

"I heard that if Lincoln wins, the southern states threaten secession," said Willie.

Grateful for the subject change, I said, "Is it that bad?" Of course, I knew it was.

"It appears so," Robert said. "There is talk about a separate union. The Confederacy."

"That's dreadful," said Sara. "All so they can work humans like animals."

"Well," said Robert, "one could blame the north for that phenomenon."

"How so?" asked Nate. I gave him a warning eyebrow. Don't mess with history, buster.

Willie answered. "The industrial advancement of the northern states, particularly in the case of factories that spin cotton and weave cloth, has created a greater need for raw material."

"The only way to meet the demand for cotton is to increase the workforce, thus the need for slaves," added Robert.

"Couldn't you meet that demand by hiring free men," said Nate, his smile gone, "black or otherwise?"

"We're talking about the need for an enormous amount of manpower, impossible to manage, not to mention a centuries old tradition."

I reached under the table and took Nate's hand, squeezing it gently. He caught my eye and understood. We couldn't get involved. Plus, his hand felt really good in mine.

"Did I not hear that your family runs a cotton plantation in Virginia, Robert?" said Willie. The mood at the table darkened.

"Indeed," Robert said.

"How many slaves does it take to run it?" Sara asked.

"My uncle owns sixty."

A small gasp escaped from Sara's lips. I tensed, and could see by the scowl on Nate's face that he didn't like what he'd heard either.

"But, I am not my uncle. Let's remain clear on that."

Thankfully, our conversation was interrupted by the arrival of the speaker. The host of the evening called us to attention. "May I introduce to you, Senator Charles Sumner."

The audience rose and applauded loudly as a gentleman dressed in a tweed suit limped carefully to the podium with the help of a wooden cane. I leaned towards Nate.

"He once spoke against slavery with a speech called The Crime against Kansas. A congressman from South Carolina beat Sumner with his cane until he was unconscious. Can you believe it? That's why he limps now. "

Nate shook his head. I continued, "This beating became a

symbol in the north of southern brutality. I'm sure we'll hear about it tonight."

Nate grinned. "How do you know all this?"

"I told you, American History is my best subject."

The applause died down and everyone took their seats. The crowd's anticipation for the coming presentation was evident. Charles Sumner would not disappoint. He cleared his throat and began, "To quote Ralph Waldo Emerson, who, I see is kind enough to attend tonight, 'An immoral law makes it a man's duty to break it....'"

A four-piece band set up after the lecture.

"What's happening now?" I asked.

Sara clapped her hands. "A dance."

A dance?

Willie asked me for the first one. "You look lovely, Cassandra," he said with a big grin, "but I have to confess, I kind of feel like I'm dancing with my brother."

I smacked him playfully. He continued, "Though I will admit to having thought that 'Casey' was a bit effeminate."

"I knew I was going to get caught in my charade sooner or later."

"Is that why you brought your brother this time?"

Hey, good idea. "Exactly."

"It's a good thing I was so nice to you. I'd hate to have been guilty of beating up a girl."

I looked up at him, suddenly wanting to ask a question I'd been wondering for a long time. "Why are you so nice to us? You and your whole family? We work for you but you treat us like peers."

"Ah, well, for one thing, the Good Book teaches us that all men and women are created equal, even ones that come and go without explanation."

"How do you know we aren't planning to rob you or harm you in any way?"

"I suppose if you were going to, you would have done so all ready. It's not our place to judge. Besides, we're commanded to entertain strangers because by doing so we may be entertaining angels unaware." He smirked. "Are you an angel?"

I laughed out loud. "Hardly."

Reluctantly I gave Willie over to one of his admirers, but didn't have to wait long before Robert approached me. I let him lead me to the dance floor, but not before throwing a beseeching look Nate's way. Besides, I'm not a great dancer. It's one thing to fake it with Willie but another with the likes of Robert Willingsworth.

"You are adorable as always, Miss Donovan." He held my waist delicately, twirling me across the dance floor. "Or may I call you Cassandra?"

Um. I really wanted to avoid unnecessary familiarity, but it seemed rude to say no. "You may, Mr. Willingsworth."

"And you may call me Robert." Robert seemed intent on staring longingly at my eyes. I responded by staring over his shoulder, gulping. I was unaccustomed to unabashed admiration.

Willie had lost no time in asking a pretty little blond to dance, and winked at me when they swirled by. Nate and Sara sat at the table alone. When I caught Nate's eyes, I tried to signal that he should ask her to dance. Amazingly, he complied, though I could tell that, like me, ballroom dancing was a foreign sport for him. Once they were on the dance floor, I pointed them out. Maybe Robert needed to see Sara with someone else before he'd clue into what he was missing.

"Look, Robert. Don't Nate and Sara look good together?" He grunted softly. On a roll, I kept going. "Sara, she's quite something. You'd be amazed at how excellent she is at managing a busy household. I would die if I had to do all the work she does with her mother bed resting. And all those children. She will make a terrific wife to some lucky man one day." Hint, hint.

"Indeed." He looked at me pointedly. "As will you."

Yikes! Just then Nate cut in. "Do you mind if I take a turn with my sister?"

Take a turn? He was picking up nineteenth century lingo.

"Certainly." Robert barely concealed his annoyance, but graciously offered to partner with Sara.

"Thank you," I said, once I was in Nate's arms.

"You looked uncomfortable."

"Indeed." I smiled up at him.

"Indeed." He smiled back. "You know, you surprise me, Casey."

"What do you mean?"

"You're nothing like I thought you were, back at school."

"Which was?"

"I don't know, quiet, boring, uninspired."

Quiet, I could deal with. Boring? Uninspired? That stung.

"And now?" I said, very interested in his answer.

"Obviously, the opposite." The corners of his mouth lifted slightly. My belly filled with happiness.

"You're not a bad dancer," I said after a comfortable pause.

"Isn't this how it all started?"

"What do you mean?"

"With a dance. How we ended up here. Together."

Oh. "We will get back, Nate. I don't know why it's taking so long, but we will get back."

Confession: Nate was intoxicating. Being this close to him, his hand in mine, well, my knees quivered. And the way he looked at me?

"Robert and Sara are watching us." I pointed out. "Remember, we're brother and sister."

Something had changed between us. Our chemistry was

sparking, and I could tell he felt it, too. I should have been ecstatic but I knew that nothing could ever happen between us here, because, for one, if word got out that we weren't siblings we'd be in big trouble (we were sharing a cabin!)

Also, I was certain that when we got home everything would return to the way it was before. I'd go back to hanging out with Lucinda, and he'd go back to his football buddies and Jessica. And I couldn't forget the reason Nate was here with me in the first place.

"Do you think your buddies got a good laugh?"

"What?"

Oh, how soon they forget. "The dare."

Nate lowered his head. "My only regret is that it took a dare to get me to dance with you." Shields up! Shields up! That had to be the sweetest thing any guy had ever said to me. All the more reason to go into self-protect mode.

"Let's not complicate things any more than they already are."

His back stiffened. "Is that what we're doing?"

"Complicating things?" I spouted. "I can't imagine a more complicated situation."

When the band announced that they were about to perform the last dance, our table prepared to leave. Nate helped me with my shawl before Robert could get to it. Sara and Willie said good-bye to their friends.

Robert approached me. "My dear Cassandra, I do hope to see you again soon. Perhaps I will call on the Watson family some-time and see you there?"

Was he asking me out? I sneaked a glance at Nate and his expression was grim. Perfectly brotherly. "I suppose so."

I was nervous, and I didn't want to be rude. "But, Nathaniel and I aren't sure how long we will be staying."

Nate broke in. "We're a bit transient that way."

Just as we got to the front door someone charged inside shouting, "Fight! Fight! A group of Southies picked a fight!" We ran outside to a nasty scene: a brawl had broken out. The oil street lamps didn't shed much light, but the moon was full. About a dozen men were throwing fists.

"Willie," Sara shouted, "go get the carriage."

"Oh no!" I grabbed Nate's arm. "Look!" Samuel Jones was in the fray. "Samuel!" I yelled. "Samuel!" For a moment he turned towards me. Eyes wide with fear, blood on his face. Then he was gone.

And so was Nate. I spun around and his familiar form wasn't behind me or to either side. Then I caught a glimpse of him in the mob. The only tall, white guy in the mix, he wasn't hard to miss.

"Nate! Are you crazy?" I couldn't believe him. "Nate! Stop!" I had no choice but to run into the mob after him. I pressed myself through muscular sweaty bodies, no easy feat with my annoying hooped skirt. I managed to grab hold of Nate's sleeve and tugged hard. "Nate! Stop it right now! This is NOT your fight!"

Maybe not, but the guys in the mob didn't know that. My distraction gave one of the guys the opportunity to punch Nate in the gut. He buckled over and groaned.

"Nate!" Despite my big hoop skirt bending half way up to the sky, I pulled him out of the crowd, almost free of it when I felt my head explode. I'd taken an elbow to the cheek. A warm, fuzzy blackness followed by mad throbbing overwhelmed me. My eyes swelled with tears.

I heard Willie's voice calling, "Cassandra! Nathaniel!" I felt his hand in mine as he led me and Nate back to the carriage. "You've been hurt," he said.

"I'll be all right." I actually felt like throwing up.

Nate held his stomach but had his breath back. He bent over to examine my face. "It didn't break the skin, but it's bruising."

The police arrived with bats in their hands, and started pounding on the backs of the men in the mob.

"Get in the carriage!" Sara poked her head out of the window. Nate helped me in and Willie jumped in the front, snapping the reins. The sudden jerk of the horses thrust me against Nate. I didn't have the energy to right myself. Nate didn't seem to mind. In fact he put his arm around me. In a brotherly fashion, of course.

"I hope Samuel is okay," Sara said, holding a handkerchief to her face. She was white as a sheet and clearly shaken. Nate's lips pulled into a tight line, anger simmering behind his eyes. The ride back to the farm was quiet; we were too upset to say much.

On our return, Sara offered to tend to my cheek. I just wanted to be alone.

"I'll be fine Sara. I'll put a cold cloth on it in the cabin." She and Willie stared after me and Nate with worried looks.

Once in our cabin, Nate started the fire to get rid of the chill. "That really sucked," he said.

I poured cool water from the pitcher into the bowl and dipped a cloth into it. After wringing it out I pressed it against my cheek. Nate saw me wince.

"Casey, I'm sorry."

"It's not your fault."

"I shouldn't have jumped in. I wasn't thinking. I'm really out of my element here."

The truth. He wasn't a traveler and he didn't belong here. I had to get him back, and then somehow forget all about this magical time we'd had together. Behind the sheet, I slipped off my hoop skirt, but kept my dress on. I crawled under the covers, exhausted. The throbbing in my cheek subsided, but sleep escaped me. I twisted and turned, frustrated that sleep wouldn't come. I needed an emotional respite from the drama of the evening. Plus, getting through the workload of the next day without sleep would be horrible.

I was awake when the night sky lightened and the rooster crowed. Ugh. How would I make it through this day? I heard Nate mumble and groan and throw off his blankets. He yawned as he stoked the fire. I splashed my face with cold water; the sting on my cheek reminded me of the night before. My stomach lurched, first at the thought that Samuel might be in trouble and then because I was certain that Nate couldn't wait to get away from all this. From this and from me.

Nature called, and I opened the door to head for the outhouse, but jumped back, stifling a yelp. Samuel had spent the night leaning up against our door. "Sorry to startle you, Miss Cassandra," he said with a coarse and raspy voice. His left eye was swollen almost shut and his split lip had dried blood.

"Samuel, come in out of the cold." Nate had jumped up when he heard Samuel's voice, and now he helped him inside, leading him to sit on the edge of his bed. I could tell by the way Nate's eyes narrowed and his jaw tightened that the sight of Samuel's beating made him angry. I soaked a cloth with water from the washbowl and handed it to him. He pressed it against his lip.

"What were you doing outside our door, Samuel?"

"I'm really sorry to disturb you. I meant to be gone before you arose. Your front door's opposite the wind."

"But, why didn't you sleep in the loft?" That was where he usually slept.

"Cobbs doesn't like black men. I probably shouldn't have come back here, but the Watson's are good people, and I don't have anywhere else to go just yet."

"What happened last night, Samuel?" Nate said.

"Slave hunters from the south. They're after runaway slaves."

Now that the blood was cleared from his mouth, I handed

Samuel a cup of water to drink. "I thought you were going to Canada. You would be safe there."

He gulped the water down and mumbled while wiping his face with his sleeve, "Uh, well, I'm waiting for my brother."

"You shouldn't waste any time leaving," I said. "The Watson's will help Jonah when he gets here. It's too dangerous for you."

"You can stay here in our cabin for now, Samuel," Nate said. "Rest up. We'll tell the Watson's that you're here."

"Thanks. You are too kind."

We almost made it to the house, too. I felt the dizziness, just as I spotted Cobbs out of the corner of my eye. I grabbed Nate's hand and pulled him frantically behind the hedge as we both began to spiral into bright white. I hoped Cobbs hadn't seen us vanish into thin air.

NINE

A DISCO BALL INSTEAD OF SUNRISE, wallflowers instead of a winter garden.

We were back in the gym, dancing the slow dance. Once again I was in my yellow knee length dress, Nate in his handsome suit and crisp white shirt. Only the telltale dark rings under his eyes confirmed that I hadn't imagined what we'd just gone through. Oh, and the stubble. I wondered how he would explain that. Lucinda stood against the wall where I had left her, with a big I'm so happy for you, grin. Tyson and Josh stood by the punch bowl laughing at their buddy dancing with the geeky girl. Jessica had her arms around Craig the sophomore, but I could see fury in her eyes. We were only mid song. I closed my eyes, trying to graft together what had just happened to the reality of me now dancing with Nate at a high school dance.

Nate breathed in sharply, "Wow. Did that really... did we really...?"

"You can't tell anyone."

"This is freaking unreal."

"Promise me."

"Were we really, uh, just there?'

"Promise me!"

"It's okay. I promise." Then he pulled me in close, like an embrace. I caught my breath. Didn't he know that everyone was watching? The song ended and he casually brushed my cheek with his lips.

A kiss? "Good bye, Cassandra."

I couldn't bring myself to look away. He hesitated a moment, and when I turned, I could sense him watching me as I walked back to Lucinda.

"What was that?" Lucinda said, shocked.

"Did he actually kiss you?"

"It was just a gentleman's kiss. It didn't mean anything."

"A gentleman's kiss?" Lucinda almost shouted. "What the heck is that?"

I shrugged, staring at the floor. I felt like I'd just walked away from a bad car wreck, physically sound but clearly emotionally traumatized.

"Did you see Jessica's face?"Lucinda sounded triumphant.

"No, I missed that."

I glanced over at the jocks. Nate was rubbing his eyes. Tyson punched him playfully in his arm. Jessica was giving him an earful, shouting, "If they dared you to jump off the roof, would you?"

"You looked like you were having an intense conversation," Lucinda said, her eyes bright with anticipation for juicy gossip.

"What were you two talking about?"

"It was a dare. The guys dared him to ask me to dance."

"Oh." She grimaced. "That bites."

Jessica dragged Nate to the middle of the gym, draping her skinny arms around his neck, forcing him to slow dance with her even though it wasn't a slow song.

"I'm not feeling well," I said.

"Actually," Lucinda said, "you don't look that great."

I was surprised she didn't notice the dark rings around my eyes. Must have been the lighting, the space against the wall was fairly dark and shadowy.

"I'm going to call my mom to come get me," I said.

"Uh, okay. I think I'll go say hi to Ashley."

"Sure. I'll see you tomorrow."

"Yeah, and I'll help you beat Nate up," Lucinda said, trying to cheer me. I watched Jessica take Nate's hand and I felt sick to my stomach. I chose an exit as far away from the punch bowl as possible.

I spent the night and the whole next day sleeping. My mother came up often to check on me, offering me food and wanting to take my temperature. I told her it was the flu and I would be better in time for school in the morning. Which I was, physically. Emotionally, well, I was still calling it.

I wondered if Nate would show up. I knew the toll time traveling took on a body, but I was used to it. If I begged off sick every time, I'd fail school and worry my mother. But he came. He drove into the school parking lot in his rusty '82 BMW. It was great to see him in jeans and a hoodie again. He looked tired, but hot, hot, hot. I waited by the door, wondering what he'd say to me, hoping he'd talk first, because I had no clue what to say.

He caught my eye. His mouth pulled up slightly at the corners, a sparkle in his countenance, an acknowledgment: we shared a secret. Then his eyes flitted over my head to his jock friends and he brushed by me with a little nod. No one else would have noted our brief communication.

That was it. Just like I knew it would be. I was beneath him. Lucinda and I, we were minions on the totem pole of Cambridge High. Nate, he was perched on the very top. I dragged myself through class, feeling particularly beat up after English. It was just like old times; Nate never even looked back at me once.

Okay, I didn't expect us to be best friends, but surely some level of friendship would be permissible? Not with Jessica around, I supposed.

"So, Casey," said Lucinda when the lunch bell rang. "I just passed the cafeteria. The football team's there." She was sensitive enough not to mention him by name.

"I had a bit of the flu this weekend. I don't think my stomach's up to the smells."

"Ah." Lucinda said, understanding. "Okay, we can skip the caf today."

"I packed a lunch," I said. "We could share?"

Lucinda nodded and we headed towards the south stairwell in the old part of the building where we could eat alone and I would be safe from any unwanted Nate sightings. We stopped at the window on the second floor where we could see a group of freshmen boys outside, smoking on the other side of the fence.

"Isn't that your brother?" Lucinda asked. I recognized his tall, moppy head.

"It looks like it." He puffed on a cigarette like an old pro and I shook my head. "He's smoking?"

He was dressed as usual in punk black like the other boys, some with hats, most of them with piercings.

Lucinda and I sat on the top step. I pulled a small plastic container from my brown bag. Butterscotch pudding, my comfort food. I savored small spoonfuls, though it didn't do much to ease the pain. I had let myself like a boy and he didn't like me back. I understood now why there were so many popular songs about heartache. I wiped a stray tear from my cheek. Salty tears didn't go well with butterscotch.

"Oh, Casey." Lucinda's eyes squished together in sympathy. "He's a jerk and not worth your trouble."

"Luce, there's something I haven't told you."

"Go on." She took half my sandwich and started eating.

"Remember the dance?"

"Where the boy in question danced with you on a dare?" she said with a full mouth. "Yeah, I remember."

"We went, uh, back."

"Back? What do you mean?" I widened my eyes as if that helped to explain it.

"I mean we went *back*."

Lucinda let out a little scream. "No way!"

I told her the Spark notes version of our time there.

"You slept in the same cabin!" She crossed her arms with indignation. "And he ignores you now? He's more of a jerk than I thought."

I didn't want to believe it, but it was true. "It hurts more than I imagined it would, you know?"

"Oh, Casey." Lucinda wrapped her arms around me, careful not to touch any skin, and squeezed. I was lucky to have a friend like her.

I went straight home after school. No guy watching for me—too painful. My heart wasn't made of stone. In fact, I was pretty sure it was bleeding and that blood might start leaking through my pores.

Tim was in the living room, playing some video game where he shot and killed stuff. "Hey, Tim." No answer. "Tim." Nothing. I plopped down on the couch beside him. "Tim!"

"What d'you want?"

"I saw you smoking today."

"So?"

"Do Mom and Dad know?"

"No, and how would Dad know anything?" Army men and weird looking creatures fell to the ground, blood everywhere.

"That's gross." Nothing. "Fine, don't talk to me, but I'm telling Mom."

"So, tell her."

"Fine." Mom came home and I helped her make supper. Pasta. Quick and Easy. I didn't tell her about Tim's new smoking habit, though I didn't know if I was doing him any favors. Instead, I brought up the subject of Dad.

"Do you ever, you know, think about Dad?"

"Oh, I'm sorry, Casey, I forgot to ask. Did you have a good time when you went out with him the other day?"

"Yes, but I mean, do you think of him? Do you miss him?"

Mom's stricken look made me regret bringing it up. "I'm sorry our troubles affect you kids, Casey. But what's done is done."

I pressed. "Can't things be undone?"

"Some things can." Then she sighed. "And some things can't."

Somehow I managed to get through the rest of autumn without falling into a total depression. The good thing was I hadn't traveled since the dance. The bad thing was I still had to see Nate every day at school. If my Nate radar had been in full gear at the beginning of the school year when I was merely crushing, it was now on total hard-core over-drive. As much as I told myself to forget him, I found myself constantly on the look-out. It was maddening. At least Jessica kept out of my face. Had Nate talked to her? The thought of him coming to my defense offered a sprinkle of happiness in an otherwise joyless existence.

I passed by the open door of the drama room and watched for a moment as the acting class had dress rehearsal. It gave me an idea. After school I took the bus to a costume shop. A bell rang overhead when I entered and a kindly looking woman with large deep-set eyes and curly gray hair greeted me.

"I'm looking for something nineteenth century-ish." Actually, I couldn't believe I hadn't thought about this before; maybe because I only had to worry about boy's clothing, which was pretty easy to find.

"A theme party?" she asked, but didn't wait for an answer. She took me to a rack at the back of the room. Gold mine.

"These dresses are great," I said, already planning to stock up. I chose two that looked like they would fit me, paid the lady and told her I didn't need a bag. I folded the dresses carefully and stuck them in my backpack. It felt great. I was a good Girl Scout. I was prepared. Next time, as long as I had my backpack on, I would be ready.

The next day I broke my own personal policy about researching people I've met in the past. It was generally best not to know what happened to them. Especially if they started to mean something to me.

I used my spare period to go to the school computer lab; I wanted to look up Samuel Jones. Did he make it to Canada? Google was still thinking when Nate walked in. He saw me, lifted his chin in a slight nod, and chose a computer where he could sit with his back to me. Every time I saw Nate, the lump in my gut throbbed with pain. I tortured myself by reliving the entire experience we had shared in the past together, and how sweet it had been to have him all to myself, even though it had been against his will. Kind of like a prisoner. My prisoner.

But now, I was the prisoner. It was worse now than before, because he knew. And it bugged me. He owned a little—no, a big part of me that I didn't want just anyone to have. I couldn't stay in this room with him, and besides, my online search came up empty. I slipped my backpack on and carefully slid my chair away from my desk. I didn't want Nate to witness my getaway. He'd figure out I left because of him and I didn't want to give him that satisfaction.

It wasn't meant to be. Dizziness kept me from walking out of the room and I was thrown into brightness. One can't help what one can't help but I could feel sorry for myself and so I did. Good and sorry. I made my way to my stash and put on the dress I had bought at the costume store. It wasn't as authentic looking as I'd first thought, but it would do. I removed other items from my pack that I might need another time: a bag of raisins, cashew nuts, tampons, and put them into one of the burlap bags.

I took a short cut straight to the Watson farm. No sense wasting time trying to find a new home away from home. I wracked my brains for another excuse and hoped that Sara's good nature and patience hadn't worn out when it came to me.

When I got there, I knocked timidly on the kitchen door. "Hello?" I wasn't the only one having a meltdown. Sara sat at the table, weeping into a handkerchief.

"Sara? What's wrong?" Then a darker thought. "Is it Samuel?"

She muffled a groan and shook her head. She must be pretty upset, because she didn't even lay into me about disappearing again. "No," she said finally, "nothing so selfless as that. It's my birthday! I'm eighteen and un-married with no prospects in sight."

Wow. How times have changed. I pulled her into a hug and let her cry it out. "Robert keeps coming around, but not to see me. He's looking for you, Cassandra."

"I'm really sorry, Sara. I know you like him and I don't know if this helps, but I don't like him at all. And to be honest, there's something about that man I don't trust. I think you could do better."

She paused to consider this. "Really?"

"Really." She seemed somewhat comforted. "Well, I don't know if that's true or not, but God Bless you for saying so." After she was composed, I asked her again about Samuel.

"I don't know what happened to him, just disappeared, like you! Why do you keep leaving without saying good-bye?"

"Sara, I'm sorry, I really am." I decided against another lie. "I can't tell you why I have to leave, but I'm asking you, as a friend, just to trust me. If I could tell you, I would."

"You have always been a girl of mystery, Cassandra. That's why Robert is attracted to you and not me." She let out a stuttered breath, that kind you do after a good cry. "I'm reliable and boring and not at all pretty." She put the handkerchief to her nose and blew.

"Sara, there's nothing wrong with being reliable. Most people consider that a good thing. You're certainly not boring and I think you are very pretty. You just have to wait for the right man to come along."

"Well, maybe you're right. Self-pity accomplishes no good thing." She looked over my head and then around the room. "Where's your brother?"

"Oh," I let my eyes flutter as I dug for a great explanation. I blanked. "Uh, he didn't come back with me this time."

Sara shook her head and smiled softly. "You are the strangest family." I nodded. "Well, you shouldn't stay in the cabin alone. Go get your things. You can stay in my room with me." She wiped crumbs off the table into her hand and brushed them into the sink. "If you'll excuse me, I'm going to go freshen up."

I watched her leave, but I didn't have a chance to take her up on her offer to stay. One tunnel of light later, I was back in the computer lab, staring at the back of Nate's head. Why couldn't our trip have been this short? Then I wouldn't have had time to fall so hard for him. He pushed his chair out and stood. He hesitated then, having made a decision, and turned to acknowledge me. I think he meant to make it short and sweet but he stared at me for several moments.

I knew what he saw. Two dark rings under my eyes. He knew I'd just traveled. He opened his mouth as if he was about to say something, but changed his mind. He glanced away, and walked out the door.

TEN

ENGLISH. WHO KNEW IT could be so cruel? Mr. Turner wrote frantically on the chalkboard, *The Tempest*, then the word "Tragicomic." With finger to chin, he scoured the faces in his class, a habit he had when looking for someone to call on. I kept my face down, but I must've had a beacon on my head that shouted Pick Me, I'm not wretched enough.

"Miss Donovan, could you explain to us the meaning of tragicomic."

Everyone swiveled to hear me. I thought Nate would remain facing forward, but it seemed suddenly he was interested in what I had to say. Another time, another place, I would've been up for this scrutiny. As it was I felt my cheeks grow crimson and my throat constricted.

"Casey?" Mr. Turner would not be ignored.

"Um, well, I think it means that while the play ends happily the road to the end is often tragic."

Much like my life. I can only hope for a happy ending of some sort, but my journey was full of comic tragedy. Mr. Turner hurriedly scribbled something on the board. He turned back to us again with finger to chin.

"Mr. Mackenzie, can you elaborate?" Nate cleared his throat.

"Sometimes the tragic situations lead us to believe it will be something other than a happy ending."

Like us? We shared a tragic situation (sort of) and it didn't end up happy. Was this a type of coded message from him to me? Mr. Turner spent the rest of the class unpacking the mysteries of *The Tempest*, ending with an assignment: one thousand word essay on the many themes of this Shakespearean tragic comedy. No time like the present. I headed for the library to work on my essay. Let's just say I wanted to get it over with. I didn't even care about my grade. It would've helped if I could concentrate. I couldn't stop thinking about Nate and how he'd answered Mr. Turner's question. Was he trying to tell me, without actually talking to me, that I should just get over it? (ie: get over him). That my life was a tragic comedy?

I was way too consumed with Nate. I actually felt like I could smell his cologne.

The empty seat beside me moved and I knew why I had picked up his musky scent. Nate sat down. "I've been looking for you."

"Funny, because it seems like I'm in your space all the time and yet you don't seem to see me."

"I know. I've been a jerk."

I wouldn't argue with that.

"Okay, you found me. What do you want?"

"I know you've been back."

I examined my fingernails. "So?"

"So, how are they? Did you find out what happened to Samuel?"

"Nate, those people have been dead for a hundred and fifty years."

"Are they dead to you?"

I sighed. "No." I wished I had a fingernail file. "No one knows what happened to Samuel. He disappeared the same day we did. I can't find any info on him or his brother on the internet. They were born slaves, so there's no record of their births. And Jones is a common surname."

Nate ran a hand through his hair. His face was troubled and I found myself wanting to comfort him, but I was the one in need of comforting here, not him.

"Maybe you're used to this, Casey, but it's been so strange for me. It took me a couple weeks just to process what had happened, and to be honest I was scared to be around you."

"That's okay." So what if you broke my heart in the process.

"It's just that you and I, we hang in different crowds. It's not that..."

"Nate, it's fine," I lied. "I get it. I knew this would happen all along. Don't worry about it."

"I'm sorry, Casey. I just wanted you to know."

I watched him leave. His swagger, the way he tossed his head to brush his hair from his eyes, how he thrust his fists into his front pockets—all familiar and endearing traits that make Nate, Nate. A deep ripping pain wrenched my gut and I all but muffled a moan and let my head drop onto the table.

His musky cologne stayed behind to taunt me. I remembered the first time I'd laid eyes on Nate Mackenzie, only a year and a half ago. Before Nate, I was perfectly happy. Well, except for the time travel part. My parents were together, their relationship seemed fine, Tim was a normal, bug catching seventh grader who never showered. I'd had little crushes along the way. Jimmy Fells in second grade. He had greasy hair and picked his nose. Not sure what the attraction was there, just another sign I was on my way to loser-dom. Sixth-grade I did somewhat better. Patrick Wiseman, the boy with the perfect name because he was just so smart. I could hardly understand him when he talked. Warm brown eyes and a dusting of freckles on his nose. His family moved to California the next summer, but by then I was over him. I don't know if he even knew that I had crushed on him.

Then there was Nate. He'd arrived half way through last year, at the semester break. By then all the girls had gotten the stats on all the boys and visa versa, and you either had a boyfriend/girlfriend or you didn't. In January, Nate was new blood on the market. Jessica had promptly dumped her then same-grade boyfriend, Jed, and well, before too long, she and Nate were a couple. I didn't know much about his family except that his father was a pilot who was transferred from Toronto to Boston. His mother worked in real estate and his older brother, John, was in the Canadian army. I'd heard he'd been shipped off to Afghanistan.

I'd first really noticed him in the cafeteria line up. Actually, Lucinda had seen him first and pointed him out, whispering, "New guy." I was immediately smitten. I couldn't take my eyes off of him and when he walked past our table, I accidentally knocked my purse on the floor. He had to set his tray on our table to help me pick up my things. I'd felt like an idiot. He could have just laughed and kept walking. I'd also bent down to scoop up my things—thankfully, just my cell phone and wallet had fallen out and not a pad or tampon. I would have died on the spot. As it was, well, our faces came within inches of each other. We were so close I saw the freckle just under his right eye.

He'd smiled, handed me my cell and my wallet, picked up his lunch tray and taken a seat at the jock table. He didn't know my name, didn't ask. But I was in love. Or rather, I was in deep, murky infatuation. Now, I thought I was in love.

And I wanted to kick myself. *Snap out of it, Casey. It could never work.* He knows all about me, and can't deal with it. The full truth of it hit me like wrecking ball: if Nate couldn't handle it, no guy could. I was destined to be ALONE forever. Once any guy found out the truth he'd hightail it out of my stupid dual track life. I was cursed! I felt like dying.

As I headed for my algebra class I had a foreign thought. If I couldn't die, then I would go home. I'd never skipped school before and the idea sent thrilling chills down my spine. I had my backpack and my purse. If I followed the kids heading to the gym, I could wait to be the last to enter, then at the final moment, slip behind the building out of sight. I was an expert at stealth. It would be simple. My heart raced a little, and the surge of adrenaline made me feel alive again.

But like any drug (so I've heard), the high was short lived and disappointing. I just missed the next bus, so by the time I finished the walk home I felt limp with fatigue. My house felt cavernous. I closed the front door behind me, clicking the lock shut. I just stood there, shell-shocked. The drabness of the gray afternoon was unwelcoming—the silence, piercing, tomb-like. I had to choose, right to the sofa, or straight ahead and up the stairs to my bed. I just wanted to lie down. My body felt heavy and lifeless like a big sandbag. Right, to the sofa took less effort. Like a zombie I walked over to it and let my dead weight fall.

Now I had another choice. Cry or sleep. I didn't have any tissues handy and lacked the energy to go get some, so I defaulted to sleep. It took surprisingly little time to doze off. I awoke to the sound of knocking on the door. Who could that be? I sat up and put my hand to my hair. A freaky, fuzzy mess. I peeked into the mirror in our entrance before grabbing the doorknob. Hideous.

Lucinda, with a bag in her arms, pushed by me. "This is called an intervention." She went right for the living room and plopped the bag on the coffee table.

"You missed school this afternoon. I was worried."

"Ah, Lucinda," I said, feeling guilty. "It's no big deal. I'm fine, really."

"You've not been the same since the dance, and since it was my idea to go, I sort of feel responsible."

"It's not your fault," I said. Lucinda pulled goodies out of the bag. "We have pretzels, soda and," she presented a DVD with fervor, "the first season of LOST. Just to remind you that you could have worse problems."

I chuckled. "This is really sweet, Luce. Thanks. But I might not be great company."

"That's okay. I'll take what I can get."

It worked for a while. I mean, Jack isn't bad to look at, and Kate's life is more of a train wreck than mine. It's true that misery loves company.

"She reminds me of you, Casey," Lucinda said.

"Well, I guess the curly hair thing is like mine."

"And she's pretty and you're pretty."

"I don't look anything like her," I countered.

"Yes, you do, except your eyes are more hazel than green. And your face is more heart shaped than hers." She popped a pretzel in her mouth. "And I think you're taller."

"But besides all that," I said. "I look just like her?"She looked at me and laughed.

Lucinda left when my mother got home from work, and I actually felt a little better. "Where's Tim?" Mom asked while pulling pots out for dinner.

"I don't know." I'd forgotten all about him. "He didn't come home after school."

I reached for our land line and dialed his cell. "He's not picking up."

Mom and I ate in the living room while watching the news. This was something we never did when Dad lived with us. We always ate together, the four of us, at the table. My mom used to say we needed to regroup as a family and share about our day. This was important to her, or at least it used to be. Now, when we'd try that, the strain of keeping up conversation long enough to finish our food was too difficult. Watching TV eliminated that pressure.

Tim still hadn't come home when the news ended. At seven o'clock, there was another knock at the door. Curious, I followed my mother as she opened it. Mom sucked in her breath and I bit my lip.

Tim had come home. Escorted by the police.

ELEVEN

"EVENING, MA'AM," THE OFFICER greeted my mother. Her stunned expression explained her lack of ability to respond. He pointed to Tim. "This here is your son?"

"Y-yes, he is. What's the problem?"

"Your son was in the company of a young man caught stealing cigarettes from the convenience store off the highway. Because he was not involved directly and because it is his first encounter with the law, he is being handed over to you with a warning."

He nodded at Tim who then took a step towards us. Tim towered over our mother by almost a foot, but our little mom made him wither with her glare. He slunk past us and up the stairs to his room. Mom thanked the officer for bringing Tim home safely. He tipped his hat and strutted back to his vehicle. I thought she'd rush upstairs and take a strip off of Tim, but instead she went to the kitchen and picked up the phone. "Richard?" I heard her say. "You need to come over right away." She told him the whole story. I should've been angry at Tim, but instead I found myself smiling. Dad was coming over. Though, he'd plan to come the next day anyway, because it was my birthday. With all the drama going on in my life, I hadn't even had a chance to think about it.

Mom marched upstairs and instructed Tim to come down and wait with her in the living room.

"Mom," he started, but Mom shut him up fast with a stern, "Wait until your father gets here!"

Know that saying—a watched pot never boils? That's what it felt like waiting for Dad. Mom wouldn't let Tim leave the room. And she wouldn't let us watch TV. Just stretched out, thin, jittery silence. I wasn't the one in trouble so I slipped up to my room. I couldn't really concentrate on anything, though, what with Tim's troubles and my own problems. I found my eyes glued to the window, watching for Dad. When his Passat finally turned into our drive, I lunged for my door and down the stairs. He wore a dress shirt, tie and suit pants. His dark eyes were squished into slits and his lips pulled down sharply.

Suddenly, I didn't want to be there, and to be honest, if it were me in trouble, I wouldn't want Tim lurking around, at least not in an obvious way. I sneaked back up the stairs and sat on the top step. I was out of sight, but could still hear everything. The lecture started and I pictured Mom and Dad hovering over Tim as he slunk down in the sofa. My mother: "Are you stealing?"

"No, you heard the cop. It was Alex. I told him not to do it."

My father: "But you were with him?"

"So?"

My mother: "Are you smoking?"

"No."

Liar! He lied about smoking, maybe he was lying about stealing.

My father: "If you're not smoking, then why were you stealing cigarettes?"

"It wasn't me. Alex smokes. He's an idiot."

Silence. Mom and Dad were pondering. Did Tim have them fooled?

My mother: "Casey, get down here."

She knew I was listening. What did she want me for? I shuffled into the room, no longer excited about Dad being home and truly angry at Tim. "Casey, is your brother smoking?"

I folded my arms across my chest. Tim's eyes widened slightly, pleading. Should I tell them the truth? Would that create enough punishment for Tim to make him want to stay out of trouble? Or would he just hate me forever? Break my parents' trust or my allegiance to my brother? This was so unfair!

"Casey," my father prodded.

"I don't know." A lie. "I have no idea what Tim does with his friends. It's not like he confides in me."

And a compromise. I didn't tell them that he smoked, but I didn't say he didn't, either. Dad turned back to Tim, ran a hand over his almost bald head and breathed out loudly.

"Son, a man is only as good as his word."

Tim folded his arms over his chest and said, "Yeah, Dad. That means a lot coming from you."

Sometimes I think my brother is stupid with a capital S. Everyone sucked in a breath. The whole room seemed to empty of oxygen. Dad finally said, "Pardon me?"

My father may have screwed up, but he was still our father and deserved our respect. He didn't cheat on us.

Maybe it was the spears coming from Dad's eyes, but Tim seemed to shrink a bit. At least he was smart enough to realize he had crossed a line. He mumbled, "Sorry."

A beat. Then thankfully, Dad said, "Apology accepted. However, you are grounded for the next month."

"A month! But I didn't do anything." Mom crossed her arms.

"Would you prefer two months?" Tim squirmed but relented.

"Fine. Are we done now?"

I elbowed Tim as we went up the stairs. "If I ever do catch you smoking again, I am going to tell."

"Whatever." He sounded beaten. I hoped he had learned his lesson. But, for me it was a happy ending to an otherwise thoroughly unpleasant evening, because Dad stayed over. He slept on the sofa, but at least our whole family was under one roof, even if it was just for one night. Something about that just felt good.

I awoke to the sensational smell of French toast. In my sleepy haze I thought I was dreaming, but when I opened my eyes, the smell remained. Then I remembered— it was my birthday.

Mom surprised me. She'd gotten up early and decorated our kitchen. A Happy Birthday streamer hung across the dining room window and balloons were attached to my chair.

"Wow, Mom, this is great. I wasn't expecting this."

Mom was wearing make-up, and on a Saturday morning. Also a cute little blouse. Were those new jeans? She looked good. Did she do this because Dad was here? I hoped so. She wiped her hands on a towel and then wrapped her arms around me from behind my chair, giving me a good squeeze.

"You are worth it, sweetheart." She kissed me lightly on the cheek. "Love you."

Dad came in from the living room and sat down in the chair beside me. He took my hand and squeezed it. "Happy Birthday, Casey."

"I'm so glad you're here, Dad," I gushed. Tim straggled in sheepishly, muttering birthday greetings in my direction. The sweet cinnamon scent of thick French toast filled the house and made me happy. Mom passed around the sliced strawberries, and I dished three spoonfuls onto my eggy toast, piled on real whipped cream and drizzled sweet but low-fat syrup (just to balance out the calories), all over it.

"So, are you going to get your license?" Tim asked. I saw a hint of jealousy there. He still had a year to go.

I hedged. "I'm in no hurry." Friends don't drink and drive, don't text and drive and don't time travel and drive.

"As soon as I turn sixteen, I'm getting mine."

My dad cleared his throat. "We'll see about that."

After we were finished eating, Mom brought the gifts to the table and I opened them. New jeans from Mom, a black T-shirt with a sketch of a wolf head from Tim, (at least he made an effort to get me something, and though not what I normally wear, it was kind of cool). Dad offered me a little gold box.

"Ooh, what's this?" It was the most amazing silver cross necklace, with a little diamond in the center.

"It's beautiful, Dad. Thank you."

It was delicate and smooth and cool in my fingers. He helped me put it on. "I'm glad you like it."

Afterwards, because I don't see him as much as I'd like, I hung out with Dad in the living room. Some news journal show was on TV about adoption and how people who wanted to find their birth kids or birth parents could sign up on this list, and if both parties signed up, the agency would notify you. "Have you signed up, Dad?"

He shrugged. "I'm happy with the parents I have."

"But aren't you curious? Wouldn't you like to know who your birth parents are?"

And why they didn't keep you? "Maybe they're trying to find you? Have you ever thought of that?"

I imagined Dad's poor birth mother waiting eagerly by her phone for a call from the agency. "I don't know if I want to open that can of worms," he said. "Some things are better left alone."

In the afternoon Lucinda plowed through the front door and gave me a big hug. "It's your birthday and I'm taking you to the mall!" I disliked shopping, but even though I was still wearing Sponge Bob, she wouldn't take no for an answer. "Get dressed, lazy bum!"

I broke into my birthday stash, slipping into the new jeans and tee. I wrestled my curls back with a brush, and pulled them into a ponytail. I showed off my new necklace to Lucinda. "Ooh, pretty. Your dad has good taste." The closest mall was across town and required tricky highway driving. It'd snowed the day before and though the roads were plowed and heavily sanded, it still made me nervous.

"Are you sure you're up to this, Luce?"

"Up to what?"

"Driving. In the winter," I said as we left the house. "You know, ice and sliding into ditches and all that."

"I'm not going to slide into the ditch." We got into her car. "Now buckle up."

I did, and with gritted teeth (mine) and white knuckles (mine), we eventually made it safely to our destination.

The mall was decked out for Christmas with red and green tinsel decorations and bright little white lights. Festive music pumped through the PA.

"Check out the crowds, Lucinda."

I wasn't sure why Lucinda had brought me here. She knew I didn't like close quarters with people or, for that matter, shopping.

"It's Christmas-time, Case. Loosen up. All the Christmas kiosks are up. Besides, I brought you here so I could buy you a birthday present. I want you to pick something you really like."

We lapped the first level and the second with repeated darts into various stores— clothes, shoes, accessories. I didn't think we'd agree on anything, even though it was my gift. Finally, Lucinda chose a lime and purple long-sleeved graphic tee, and held it up to my face.

"This would look so great on you!" Lucinda gushed. I just wanted the torture to end.

"Yes, I love it. Can you get this for my birthday? Please."

Lucinda didn't get the sarcasm. "See, Casey, it's worth the effort, finding just the right one." After she paid, she handed me the bag with, I admit, my really cool shirt. "Let's go to the food court. I'm starving."

We ordered two chocolate fudge sundaes and sat down. Lucinda removed a small gift bag—it had a picture of a birthday cake topped with zillions of lit candles on it—from her ginormous purse. "You already got me a gift."

"So?" Lucinda said between bites. "I wanted to get you this, too."

"Were you carrying this around with you the whole time?" I asked.

"Yup. So, open it."

Lucinda's gift was the latest Sponge Bob DVD. I laughed, "How'd you know?"

"I've known you a long time. Happy birthday, my friend."

Ah, Warm Fuzzies. The hazard with having a birthday so close to Christmas was the tendency for people to give you one gift and say Happy Birthday and Merry Christmas. It meant a lot to me that Lucinda never did that.

"So, is it true that a police car was parked outside your house last night?"

That's what happens when you live in the same place your whole life. Everyone knows your business. "How?"

She sucked on her plastic spoon and mumbled, "Facebook."

"Well, apparently Tim's made some new friends."

"They always blame the friends. What did he do?"

I swallowed a small amount of hot fudge and cool vanilla ice cream. Normally I would gobble this up, but my stomach was still bloated from brunch. "He was with someone who shoplifted. At least that's what he claims."

"You don't believe him?"

"I don't know. I want to."

"What did he steal?"

"Cigarettes."

Lucinda nodded her head knowingly. She'd seen him smoking, too. "So, did they book him?"

"That's very cop show, Luce. No, he got off with a warning."

"Lucky."

"Yeah." I pushed my half-finished sundae to the side.

Lucinda eyed it. "You don't want that?" I slid it her way. "Knock yourself out." I tightened my ponytail.

"The good part is that Dad came over last night and he and my mom talked until, like, midnight." All talk was good talk in my books, even if it was just about us kids.

Lucinda had stopped listening to me and was staring at something over my shoulder. I turned around. It was Nate and his buddies, Tyson and Josh. My stomach performed a double axel and nailed the landing. They carried trays of food and hadn't spotted us yet. Lucinda tuned back in to me. "Do you want to go?"

"What? This is a prime guy gazing opportunity for you. Josh's there."

"True. But I understand if you want to go." I thought about it. Was I going to run away every time I saw Nate? Would I let him rule my life like that?

"No, I'm fine. I'm over him." Big Fat Liar am I. Our conversation came to a standstill. The guys were about to sit at a table right in my line of vision. Then he saw me. A slight tremor of shock evident in his eyes. Did I frighten him that much? Or did he despise me now?

He surprised me by choosing a chair that faced me. I was so used to looking at the back of his head, I didn't know how to take this sudden change.

Every few minutes he'd glance up, catch my eye and quickly cut away, like he didn't want me to catch him looking at me.

"What's going on?" Lucinda said. She swiveled her chair for a better look.

"Nothing. Are you done yet?"

"Almost." Lucinda scraped at the bottom of the dish that used to belong to me, her eyebrow still raised. Nate and I kept playing the 'I'm staring at you but I don't want you to catch me' game. I knew why I was compelled to watch him. It perplexed me as to why he was having the same problem with me. He had made it pretty clear in the library that he wasn't interested.

He stood up. But not with his friends. Alone. He locked eyes with me and walked in my direction. My blood pressure dropped. Maybe I have low blood sugar. I should have finished my sundae. I could hear Lucinda gasp. He sat down beside me. I really did feel sick.

"Hi," he said. I had a sudden flashback of us riding in the Watson carriage sitting side by side. Dumb.

"Hi?"

He eyeballed the gift bag. "Looks like it's someone's birthday?"

"Um, it's mine."

"Really? You never mentioned you had a birthday coming up."Lucinda's eye's flicked from my face to Nate's.

"Well, you know, I'm kind of a private person."

He held my gaze. "Yes, I do know that. Happy Birthday."

Then two life-altering things happened at once. Jessica came up the escalator and spotted Nate sitting by me. He didn't see her, because if he had he probably wouldn't have done what he did next, a spontaneous and really dumb thing. He put his arm around me for a hug. And with the other hand, he grabbed one of mine and squeezed.

TWELVE

"THIS IS MY FAULT, I GUESS," Nate said.

What he meant was he'd done a stupid thing by touching me. Not that I travel every time someone touches me, just it seems, when he touches me.

We stood in the forest, like before, only this time he was still holding my hand.

I looked down at our interlocking fingers and fought back a big lump forming in my throat. Despite my best efforts, a runaway tear escaped down my face.

"I'm sorry, Nate." Our hands broke free.

"It's okay. I suppose you could call it a calculated risk on my part."

Then, he reached up and wiped away my stray tear with his finger. Every nerve in my body went into Fourth of July fireworks mode. He leaned forward slightly. Oh? Was he going to kiss me? The shock of this possibility caused me to jolt back involuntarily. Oh no. Now he thought I didn't want him to. (Did I? Of Course I Did!)

"Nate?" He squinted and took a step back. "Uh, I just, uh, it's nothing."

What's nothing? What's NOTHING? Was he or wasn't he? Then he bowed like a waiter, motioning with his hand for me to lead the way to my stash.

"Back to the Watsons'?" he said.

"I guess so." I was still recovering from our almost-kiss. I didn't get it. His we-run-in-different-crowds speech still rang loud and clear in my head. Did he have a change of heart? Or was he just being nice? Maybe he felt bad for ignoring me all these weeks? I mean, he still had Jessica, after all. Call me stupid. That wasn't an almost-kiss, just wishful thinking on my part.

We reached the stash and Nate politely waited outside the grove as I changed from my birthday wolf T-shirt and jeans into the dress I'd left there last time. I quickly felt for the cross necklace, relieved to find it still there. It was cold, and I had to leave my zippered jacket behind at the stash. I reminded Nate, no zippers, so he left his hoodie behind too, and pulled his T-shirt down to hide the one on his jeans. Which were also a problem, since denim, at least the widespread use, was still a decade or so away. But he couldn't very well remove those.

We made the hike to the Watson farm in silence. Mostly. Except for when I couldn't keep my mouth shut. "I guess we're back to brother and sister," I said.

He let out a long breath. I could tell he wasn't looking forward to this. Well, too bad for him. It wasn't my fault he'd touched me. Calculated risk, my butt. Next time he'd know better. It was my turn to let out a long breath. Like there would be a next time. To my surprise, the next time came the next second. Nate slipped his arm around my shoulders.

"You're shivering."

What could I say? It felt amazing, and I wanted to kick

myself. I hated that I was setting myself up for more heartache. He was just a dumb boy.

"I'm fine," I said slipping away. For a split second he had a wounded look on his face, but he quickly recovered.

Our ride to the farm came from an unwelcome source. Cobbs rode up pulling a cart.

"Well, look what we have here," he said, bringing the horse to a stop. A smarmy grin crossed his round, ruddy face. "Ain't you two the happy wanderers."

"Hello, Cobbs," Nate said coolly. "Actually, we were just on our way to the Watsons' farm."

"Of course you were." He stared at us pompously like he had the upper hand. Was he going to drive away and make us walk? Nate took the initiative and swung his leg over the back of the cart. "You don't mind us hitching a ride, I hope." He didn't wait for an answer before taking my hand and helping me in. The way he just took charge was so awesome. I felt swooning coming on.

Cobbs shook his head and clucked his tongue. "I don't get why the Watsons put up with you folks."

Someone had left an old horse blanket in the cart and Nate wrapped it around our shoulders. I was freezing, so this time I didn't resist. Our combined shivering and body heat warmed us up, and I didn't even mind the horsey smell. Try as I might, I couldn't help but enjoy snuggling close to Nate. I was definitely my own worst enemy.

The trees on the farm were bare of leaves with a thick frosting of snow. A hare hopped into the woods as we rolled down the driveway. Two of the younger kids were making snow angels on the ground. They waved when they saw us exit the cart.

"The cabin's empty," Willie said after greeting us. "You know the way. I'll tell Sara that you're here. You can join us for supper."

"Thanks, Willie," I said. "We just ate, so we won't trouble you anymore today. You can put us to work tomorrow."

"If that's what you prefer. See you in the morning."

He tipped his hat and walked to his house. The cabin was ice cold. Nate started the fire and I lit the candle. The sheet still hung between the two beds, which was a relief, and I quickly shucked myself between the covers of mine. I watched Nate start the fire in silence. It was awkward the last time we were here together because we didn't even know each other (not counting my prior near stalking obsession with Nate), this time it was awkward because we did know each other. But now there was a line drawn in the sand. Or more like a sheet that hung between us. The faded cotton symbolized how we stood with each other. I'd better stay on my side if I knew what was best for me.

Once the fire was roaring, Nate dropped onto his mattress, putting his arms behind his head.

"So, this is your life, Casey." I didn't quite know what he meant. It wasn't a question so I didn't feel a need to respond. Apparently, Nate felt like talking. "Just one big loop over and over."

I conceded, "Something like that."

"Doesn't it drive you crazy? Having your life interrupted all the time. Having to be two different people. Having to survive in a strange era?"

Wow. He'd gotten so intense.

"It drives me crazy if I let it, but it's not something I can control," I said, rolling onto my side. I could see the top of his head, from his eyes up, past the edge of the hanging sheet where it didn't quite reach the wall by several inches. "I kind of view it like someone living with epilepsy. You can't help the seizures, but you can't let them rule your life. You have to keep on living, knowing that the seizures can happen any time any place." I let out a heavy sigh. "Yes, it is hard to live two lives, having to be two different people in two different worlds, but it's not impossible. It's not the worst thing a person could live with."

Nate turned onto his side to face me. We were looking at each other eye to eye. It was kind of intimate in an eye-staring kind of way. "I've never met anyone like you, Casey."

Well, duh. "You're the strongest, bravest person I know."

What? Really? I felt myself blushing, and was glad it was fairly dark in the room. He continued, "Aren't you afraid of changing history? I mean, how do you know that you already haven't?"

Recovering from the shock of his last statement, I answered, "I used to be really afraid of that, especially after I watched Back to the Future II, when Michael J. Fox snagged the sports almanac and wrecked the space time continuum. But then I realized I am part of that history. Our future is what it is despite the fact that I'm here, maybe even because I'm here."

"I don't get it."

"When I'm in real time, my time, the past has already happened, including all the part with me in it, like now. It's a loop. So when I'm here, I know that whatever happens with me, already happened once I get home. It's part of the history."

"Aren't you tempted to try to change things? Don't you want to do something like save Abraham Lincoln before he gets shot?"

"I used to think that maybe I'm here to try to fix an injustice, undo an evil, but then I figured maybe I could just end up setting the course for an even greater injustice or a greater evil. I'm not God. It's not my place to mess with something this big."

That seemed to give him pause for thought. His eyes moved from mine back to the ceiling. I did the same. I counted four spiders.

"I do wonder why, though. Why do I travel? Why me? Is it just a weird quirk of nature, or is there some higher purpose?"

Five. Five spiders.

Nate didn't have an answer for that. Only more questions. "What happens if you die here?" What? Was he worried I might die? Or that if I died he'd be stuck here?

"I don't know. I just assumed that since I'm still there, I couldn't have died here."

"Are you sure?"

"No."

We were interrupted by a banging on the door. Nate jumped up to open it. It was Willie, all red faced, his hair damp and dotted with specks of snow.

"Sorry to bother you, but Cassandra, Sara needs you. Our mother is having the babe." Nate and I ran with Willie through a thick blanket of snow, bursting into the kitchen where Sara was pouring hot water into a bucket.

"Willie," Sara instructed, "keep the little ones quiet. Cassandra, come with me." She shoved a stack of towels into my arms and grabbed the large pail of steaming water. We sprinted up the wide staircase. "The midwife can't come in this storm," Sara explained. "I've never done this by myself, though between the two of us and all the babies our mothers have brought into the world, we should be fine."

Fine? I'd never seen anything born in my life! Not even a kitten or puppy!

"Uh, Sara," my chest tightened with anxiety. "I, uh—" Mrs. Watson's screams shut me up.

"Mother," Sara said, soothingly. "We're here. Cassandra is with us. Everything is going to be all right." Mrs. Watson's pale face glistened with sweat. She had a sheet pulled over her mountainous belly, and her legs were spread apart. I felt faint. I bit my lip and shifted my weight from one foot to the other.

"Put the towels down, Cassandra, and use one to wipe Mother's forehead."

Good. Instructions. I could wipe the woman's head. Then

another labor pain came on. Somehow Mrs. Watson found my hand and squeezed. Hard. She had a small bony hand, but boy, was she strong. I almost yelled out in pain with her. "It's coming," she said.

Oh. My. Goodness.

Sara lifted the sheet higher and I thanked God that I never had to see my own mother this way.

"I see the head, Mother. Push."

Mrs. Watson pushed and pushed. She pushed for at least a half hour but it felt like eternity to me. By the end of it my hand was crushed, but I wasn't going to complain. All of a sudden there was a baby. And blood. Lots of blood. It was all way too gross. When Sara cut the umbilical cord with a pair of sewing scissors and clipped it with a hairpin, I almost threw up.

"Get the towels," Sara commanded.

Right. Towel duty. I tossed her one, and she wrapped it around a very small and very wrinkly little creature. Sara put her finger into its mouth and then it cried. I let out a breath. Then Sara motioned with her eyes from the towels to the blood. I started mopping, too stunned by what had just happened to be freaked out by the fact that I was wiping up blood.

Sara gave the baby to Mrs. Watson and she put it to her breast. Okay, another thing I'm glad I never had to watch my own mother do. "He's beautiful, Mother," I heard Sara say. So, it was a boy. Thankfully the baby was fine, but I definitely could see why women died in childbirth.

I dropped the soiled towels in a basket and sat down on a chair near the window. My knees were shaking.

"What's he to be called, Mother?"

"I think Daniel is a nice name," Mrs. Watson said weakly. We worked together to change the sheets, tricky with Mrs. Watson still in the bed.

Then Sara instructed her mother. "You need to rest now. I'll watch over Daniel while you sleep." Mrs. Watson closed her eyes and was out before the count of three.

I followed Sara downstairs. She carried the baby, excited to show him off to his new siblings.

We were greeted with the sweet smell of toast. Nate didn't know what to do while we were busy upstairs so he had made toast. Lots and lots of toast.

"Here he is, everyone!" Sara called. All the Watson kids rushed into the living room to peek at their new brother. "Careful now," she said to the younger ones. "He's very fragile."

After a while the younger kids got bored and Sara sent them to bed, telling the older girls to help. Finally it was just Sara, Willie, me and Nate. And the baby.

"I think, if you're done with me, Sara," I said. "I will go back to my cabin."

"Of course you must be tired. Thank you so much for your help tonight."

Not like I did a lot. I took a peek at the bundle in her arms.

"Hey, Danny Boy," I whispered.

"Do you want to hold him?" Sara held him out for me. I didn't know. He seemed kind of breakable. She didn't wait for me to answer.

"Uh, okay." She helped me scoop him up and I quickly sat down in the rocking chair. I sneaked a peek at Nate and saw him grinning. He was amused by my discomfort.

"Does he make you miss yours?" Sara asked.

"Miss my what?" I said, surprised.

"Your baby brother." My baby brother? Oh yeah, the last big story. I almost forgot about my fictional family.

"Yeah, I guess."

"What's his name?"

"Whose name?" I realized I sounded like an idiot.

"Your baby brother's name?"

Tell the truth whenever you can because, that way you don't forget when you've lied about something. Also, most people get really upset when they find out you lied to them.

"My brother's name is Timothy."

"Nice Christian name."

Sara rubbed Daniel's head. "Isn't he a miracle?"

"Yes, he is." As I held him, something stirred in me, something really strange, like the desire that one day I might want to be a mother. A surprising thought, considering what I'd just witnessed. Then it struck me. How could that be? How could I be a traveler and a mother? I might be changing a diaper or pushing the stroller and "poof", disappear. I could bring the baby back in time with me. Or worse, leave it behind in the past! It would never work! It would be unsafe and unfair. I couldn't believe I'd never thought of this before. I glanced back up at Nate. He yawned.

Who would want to marry me if I couldn't have kids? I was going to be alone forever. I felt a tremble in my chest, my eyes glazed with tears.

"Cassandra?" Nate stared at me with concern. "We should get some rest."

"Okay," I said with a little hiccup as I handed the baby back to Sara. Nate and I walked back to the cabin and I couldn't keep from sniffing. His expression flipped from worry to confused, and I think he was glad to have this night finally end. So was I. Having babies makes you really emotional, I found, even if you're not the one actually having the baby.

THIRTEEN

OVER A WEEK HAD GONE BY. Shadows and lines of fatigue drew heavily on Nate's expression. He worked the farm with Willie and that awful Cobbs, and I knew it wasn't fun. It was cold hard labor, but I had to give him credit. He rose to the challenge. He said if I could take it, meaning life in the nineteenth century, then he could, too. The farm chores didn't stop just because it was winter. Cows didn't take time off of milking for the holidays. The house, obviously, lacked central heating; a good deal of energy was spent on keeping all the fireplaces lit.

I was in the kitchen stirring the massive pot of oatmeal when the door opened, flooding the heated room with a cold blast of air. Nate's head popped through, then Samuel's.

"Look who I found in the yard," Nate said with a smile. He slammed the door shut against the frigid draft.

"Samuel!" I felt like giving him a big hug, but held back. He removed his cap and nodded at me.

"Miss Cassandra." There was an uncomfortable moment, especially since the last time we had seen Samuel, he had been beaten up. Thankfully, Sara entered the kitchen and cut in.

"Samuel," Sara said after greeting him, "you're shivering. Come stand by the stove." Then she ordered her sister Josephine to add an extra plate to the table. Cobbs arrived shortly afterward and his greeting, as usual, was anything but warm. Any tension his presence might have caused was drowned out by the buzz of children's voices and Mrs. Watson's shrill attempt to calm them down.

Nate leaned in towards Samuel. "So, what've you been up to?" Samuel took a sip of coffee. "This and that. Just trying to find work and keep warm."

"Did you find your brother? Jonah?" I asked hopefully.

He shook his head. "Still can't find the youngster."

Cobbs fidgeted more than usual, his eyes darting to Samuel. The deep grimace on his face irked me. He didn't even try to hide his prejudice. He excused himself abruptly the moment his bowl had been licked clean. We all ignored his rudeness.

"Did you sleep in the loft last night?" Nate asked. I'd wondered the same thing.

"It's better for someone like me to keep moving around."

We nodded. Cobbs could cause him trouble. Plus there was that little problem of the Fugitive Act.

"Well, we're glad to have extra hands today," Sara added. "Willie had to leave early this morning for Worcester. I'm sure Nate will be happy to have your help today." After the guys left, I helped Sara clean up. Mrs. Watson buzzed around with little Daniel strapped to her chest, instructing the maid, Missy, who had just arrived, and me on which chores to attend to and when. Sara had the younger kids in the study, for school lessons.

"Why don't the kids go to school?" I asked Missy when Mrs. Watson had left the room.

"Too cold." Missy said with a sharp accent. "Too far for the young'uns to walk. 'Sides, Miz Sara is a far better teacher than that old oaf they hired."

"Old oaf, as in a man?" I inquired. "I thought teaching jobs went to women."

Missy shrugged. "Only if there isn't a man to do the job first."

Sara brought the children in for a mid morning snack, just as the door blew open. Nate stormed in out of breath, his eyes bright with concern. "Someone's taken Samuel!"

"What?" Sara and I said together.

"I can't be sure. One moment he was there and then next thing I know, he's nowhere to be found. I was scouting around the lake when I saw a man riding off in the distance. He was squat and heavy, like Cobbs, who also happens to be missing."Nate's face flushed as he told the story, his words, quick and intense. "Another man was strapped over the back of Cobbs' horse. His hands were tied behind his back. I'm sure it was Samuel. They headed toward Boston."

"Do you think Cobbs took him for reward money?" I said, nervous tension swelling up in my gut. "What if someone is there to claim him?"

"Oh no." Sara's jaw tightened. "And Willie won't return from Worcester until later this afternoon."

"Can you ride a horse?" I asked Nate. Sara looked at me sharply. First, if he was my brother, wouldn't I know that, and second, everyone around here knows how to ride a horse. I attempted to cover. "I mean, can you ride a horse, you know, since your accident?" Oh brother, another lie to remember.

Nate stared at me queerly. "Yes, I learned in Canada." Now he'd screwed up. We'd already told the Watson's we'd never been to Canada.

"You mean the horse we got from Canada."

Sara had enough of our foolishness. "Nate, take a horse and follow him." I grabbed a coat and ran after Nate.

"What are you doing?" Nate's forehead wrinkled in annoyance.

"I'm going with you."

"No you're not," he said, without looking back.

I caught up to him, pulling on his arm. "Yes, I am."

His lips formed a stiff line. "No, it could be dangerous."

"NATE!"

This was my life, not his. He was a guest on my loop. He must have seen the furor in my eyes because he stopped briefly.

"I'm the one who's supposed to be here, Nate, not you. I'm coming."

We both knew we didn't have time to waste arguing about it. We raced to the barn, and I helped Nate saddle up the closest mare. I lifted my skirt, stuck my foot in the stirrup and hoisted myself on behind Nate. I wrapped my arms firmly around his waist and off we went. If I wasn't so cold and so worried about Samuel and so stiff from not having ridden a horse in a long time, this would've been really romantic. It turned out neither Nate nor I were that great with horses. The animal could sense it and started doing that skittery thing.

"Whoa, Nellie," Nate cooed. "It's okay."

We weren't even galloping. We were cantering. It was bumpy and I bounced like a jumping bean.

"We've got to go faster, Nate!"

Nate kicked Nellie and she got the message. We took off like a shot and if I hadn't been hanging on to Nate, I would've been thrown off the back.

The road was slick with ice and every once in a while Nellie would lose her footing. I squeezed Nate so tight, I wondered if he could breathe. The branches of the bare trees began to blur and I shut my eyes tight, too.

"I see him!"

I dared to open my eyes and saw Cobb's red flannel jacket wave like a flag in the distance. He obviously didn't think he was in any danger of being caught.

"Cobbs!" Nate called out. "Stop!"

Cobbs twisted his thick neck, spotted us, then kicked his horse hard. She picked up speed and I worried we'd lose track of him. Or worse, that Samuel would fall off the back. He bounced around like a sack of flour, and I knew then that he was still knocked out.

At least I really hoped that he was knocked out and that it wasn't something worse. Like dead.

Cobbs veered off the road and into the woods. Nate urged Nellie to follow. Cobbs may have had the added burden of Samuel's body weighing him down, but he also had the advantage of better horsemanship and of knowing the area.

We did our best to keep up. Nellie's hooves sunk into crusty snow and she whinnied in protest. Nate and I had to duck under branches, and a few got caught in my hair and scratched at my face.

Nellie slowed up.

"What's the matter?" I said, my breath puffing out like little blasts of steam in front of my face.

"I can't see him. The path splits. I don't know which way to go."

"Where could he have gone? Nate, we can't give up!"

"I'm trying, Casey!"

We heard a twig crack and I spotted a flash of red. "That way!"

Nate pushed Nellie to pick up speed over a length of flat straight trail. I thought we might catch Cobbs.

Until I saw the fallen log crossing the path, just as we turned a bend.

I yelled, "Nate!"

He pulled up on the reins. Nellie made an effort to jump the oversized tree, but it was too slippery. She got her back leg caught on the log and stumbled in her landing.

I screamed.

The sky and earth spun.

I heard a thump and a groan. Was it Nate? Was it me?

My head hurt. I felt pain. That was good. It meant I was still alive. It hurt to breathe. Cutting jabs as I drew a breath in, searing pain as I let it out.

Another groan. Not mine.

"Nate?"

A shadow fell over me. Nate's face, blurry at first, came into focus.

"Casey? Are you all right?"

"I hit my head. And my ribs hurt, but I think I'm okay, nothing broken. How about you?"

Nate cradled his left elbow. "My arm. But it's not broken either, just bruised."

"Where's Nellie?"

"She's over there, in the trees. She's fine."

Ouch. Nate helped me back to my feet. He called Nellie in a quiet calm voice, inching his way to her. I let out a painful breath of relief when he grabbed her reins.

Eerie quiet. Every movement resounded like an echo chamber. Snow, trees. Silence.

Alone. A shiver crawled up my back. I was chilled and a little freaked out.

"We're not lost, are we?"

"Nah. We're on a trail. It's bound to get us to the road eventually." Nate helped me get back on Nellie. I gritted my teeth to cope with the pain, though the initial trauma had subsided. Nate swung up behind me this time. His arms pressed in against my waist as he held the reins, guiding Nellie. I leaned into his back, comforted by his warm, sturdy body.

We'd lost Samuel.

A tear trailed down my cheek and I couldn't stop a little sob from escaping.

"We can't give up," I whimpered. "We have to find him."

I felt a deep breath leave his body.

"I want to find him, too. But, what about your philosophy? Not to get involved? If we rescued Samuel, aren't we interfering? Maybe changing history?"

I didn't know. Maybe Samuel was supposed to be rescued by us.

Maybe he wasn't.

My nose was red and runny. My lips were chapped and my ears were cold. We were stuck in the forest in 1860 and we had failed to save our friend. A hard pit had formed in my gut. I just wanted to go home.

Nate had let the reins fall loose in the hope that Nellie could instinctively take us home. The farther we went, the more things looked the same. Leafless, frost covered branches, gray sky, slippery trail.

"We're just going in circles," I said. Hopelessness iced my words.

"No, we're not. Nellie will get us out."

I wished I'd mirrored Nate's confidence in our horse's capabilities. The sky turned a darker gray, and I worried that we'd be lost in the forest overnight. It'd be hard to start a fire without matches in this cold wetness. We could freeze to death if the temperature kept dropping.

Then, suddenly, Nellie found the road.

"You did it, Nellie!" I leaned forward and patted her neck. "Thank you!"

Nate gazed left then right. "Which way, Casey?"

I wasn't sure. "The sun is setting over there, so that must be the direction of the Watson's farm. We'll have to wait until we come to a road marker to know for sure."

Nate steered us west and I swallowed hard. Heading back to the Watson's meant that we had given up.

The temperature kept dropping. I pulled my jacket tighter but couldn't keep from shivering. Nate wrapped his arms snugly around me and I pressed my back into his chest. I felt his warm breath on my neck.

If it weren't for Samuel, I'd be insanely happy.

After a while I spotted a light in the distance. "What's that?"

"I don't know, but I think we'll find out."

As we got closer, we could see a small wooden building with a number of horses tied up to posts by the front door. Oil lamps shined through the windows.

"I think it's a pub."

"That's Blossom," Nate said softly.

"Who?"

"The horse Cobbs was riding."

A little flare of hope exploded in my heart. "Then he's here? Samuel must be here, too!"

"Shh," Nate cautioned. "We have to be careful."

Nate slipped off Nellie, helped me down, and then tied Nellie to a post on the farthest end. We sneaked up to a window, keeping low beneath the pane.

My heart was beating like a little bird's. We slowly lifted our heads until just our eyes were high enough to see.

The window was grimy so it was hard to make things out, but it also made it tough for the patrons to notice us, too.

The small room was dark with only candle light to illuminate it. I could see a dozen men, give or take, scattered through the tavern, some in small groups around tables, and others alone on stools at the bar. One of the loners was Cobbs.

"He's in there," I whispered.

"Can you see Samuel?"

I shook my head. "Cobbs wouldn't bring a black man in there. He must've tied him up out here somewhere."

We kept low and followed a trail to the back side of the pub. In the trees a short way was a little shack.

I pointed. "In there."

The door was padlocked. "Samuel?"

I heard movement. I knocked. "Samuel?"

"Who's there?"

It was Samuel's voice!

"Samuel, it's Cassandra and Nathaniel. We're here to help you."

The door rattled as Samuel pushed from the inside.

"It's locked," Nate said. "Wait until I find a rock."

Nate dug through the snow until he found a stone a bit larger than his fist. He slammed it against the lock.

"Nate, it's too loud!"

He struck again, but the lock didn't budge.

"Stand back, Samuel," Nate said. "I'm going to kick the door."

Then he did. Like some kind of superhero. The hinges gave way and I smiled at Nate, fully smitten by his act of courage and strength.

We worked to move the door out of the way.

"Samuel," I said as we pulled him out of the shack. "Are you okay?"

"I got a bump the size of the dome on my head, and I'm a little stiff, but otherwise I'm fine. I can't believe you did it, but thanks for coming after me."

"No time for small talk," Nate said. He was already leading us back to Nellie.

Except, how could three people ride one horse?

"Case," Nate began, "You take Samuel back to the Watsons'. I'll meet you there."

"But you don't know the way," I protested. "You take Samuel and I'll walk."

"There's no way I'm leaving you unattended, Casey."

"Uh, Miss Cassandra, if I may interrupt, Mr. Nathaniel is right. This is no place for a lady to be found alone."

"Oh, all right." I look hard at Nate. "Are you sure you'll be all right?"

Samuel spoke again. "Actually, if you don't mind, I think I'll make my own way. I'm so grateful for your help, but I can manage now on my own." He put his hand out and Nate grabbed it. He nodded politely to me, then sprinted into the woods.

"Samuel!"

"Shh, Casey. We don't want to be found out. He'll be fine. It's us I'm worried about now."

Maybe Nate was right. Maybe they were both right. I waved weakly in the direction of Samuel's fleeing form. Nate helped me back onto Nellie and we quietly trotted away.

FOURTEEN

WE HAD A CAPTIVE AUDIENCE in the kitchen after Sara made sure we'd warmed up and eaten. Now we sat around the table with mugs of hot tea in our hands.

"I can't believe it," Sara said shaking her red braids. "I'm just so glad that Samuel got away. God bless you both for what you did."

"Yes, well done," Mrs. Watson added. "No man deserves to be treated like cattle or a family pet."

"Well, Cobbs is certainly not welcomed here anymore." Willie had returned earlier from Worcester. "I can't believe I missed all this excitement."

Our recollection was interrupted by a knock at the door. Willie opened it to reveal Robert Willingsworth. Sara's eyes brightened as she joined her brother to welcome him.

"Greetings, Robert," Willie said. "What brings you this way?"

"An invitation, actually," Robert said, greeting all the Watsons before letting his eyes lock in on mine. I hated when he did that.

"Miss Donovan." He tipped his hat. "Such, a pleasure to see you again."

Sometimes, I can't believe my vanity. My hand patted at my fly away curls, and all I stewed over was how flushed my face was from the cold, then the heat, and now by him.

Robert turned to face Nate, hesitated then reached out his hand. Nate shook it limply.

"I thought I saw you both out riding today, near the tavern on route 4?"

Nate said, "You were there?"

"I was just leaving as you passed by. A shame we didn't meet a moment sooner. We could've shared a pint." He laughed. "But then again, we couldn't because you were in the company of your lovely sister."

I was stunned. Robert was at the tavern? I didn't see him when we'd peeked in through the window, though he could've had his back to us. What an unfortunate coincidence. If he'd decided to leave the tavern five minutes earlier than he had, he might've seen us break out Samuel.

"Well, we're certainly delighted that you dropped by," Sara said, smiling widely. Kind of gushing.

"Yes, the reason for my visit," Robert continued. "I would like to invite you all to a Christmas Party tomorrow night. At my estate."

At his estate. Now wouldn't that be something. Kind of a last minute invite, though. Why did I think it had something to do with his seeing us near the pub earlier?

"It would be our greatest pleasure and honor to join you, Mr. Willingsworth," Sara said.

"Tremendous. We shall see you all then."

We were soon to be surprised by another arrival. Mr. Watson had returned from London. He was larger and louder than I'd remembered. His head was still full of thick, curly, fiery-red hair. His boisterous laugh filled the house. All the Watson kids excitedly jumped on their dad to hug him. He did seem genuinely affectionate towards his much thinner and smaller wife, giving her a gentle grizzly bear hug and a long kiss on the lips. And after depositing a number of presents under the tree, he took a moment to gaze at little Daniel in the cradle.

After the initial excitement Sara introduced him to Nate and me. The last time he'd seen me, I'd been dressed like a boy. I just pretended this was our first encounter. He shook my hand warmly and said, "Welcome to the family," like he had adopted us. Which was kind of nice when you think about it, but I couldn't get past the fact that this man left his family for months at a time to fend for themselves and let his wife have a baby in his absence. They didn't seem to mind this and apparently he brought home a lot of money, so maybe that was why.

Later that night, after the candle was already snuffed out, Nate spouted off. "I don't like the way he looks at you."

"Who?"

"You know who."

He couldn't mean Mr. Watson. "Robert?" I clarified.

"Oh, it's Robert now."

"You expect me to call him Mr. Willingsworth? When talking to you? Besides, he asked me to call him Robert."

"Of course he did."

What was his problem? Was he jealous? It was pitch black so I couldn't read his face. Maybe he was jealous. This consideration brought on a wave of happy tingles. Then I remembered that he still had Jessica and of course I couldn't forget the infamous library speech.

"I just don't trust him, that's all."

"Okay, don't trust him. But we have to go to the party. We owe it to the Watsons."

"Unless..." He left the sentence hanging. I knew what he was thinking. Unless we finally went home.

ROBERT WILLINGSWORTH really did have an estate. His two story brick and stone mansion had a view of Charles River, and an enormous yard and garden. Even in the winter you could tell it was amazing. I couldn't recall seeing anything like this in the Boston I knew. The bigger question was, how did someone as young as Robert Willingsworth come into all this money?

We were in the ballroom. His house had a *ballroom*! The high ceilings were dotted with crystal chandeliers, the walls adorned with large paintings and portraits of what I assumed were important family members. A twelve-person brass band played what I imagined were the top forty tunes of 1860 interspersed with old Christmas songs I recognized.

It seemed the whole town of Boston had been invited, including the entire Watson clan. Duncan, Josephine, Charlotte and Abigail were at that odd age where you were interested in the opposite sex but pretended you still hated each other. They hung out in small groups with their friends, the boys in one, the girls in the other. Jonathon, Michael and Josiah just ran around like free birds, picking at the appetizers off the large tables that were adorned with lace cloths and ornate centerpieces at the back of the room. Mrs. Watson was at one of the tables with little Daniel in her lap, and Mr. Watson sat beside her, his big beefy arm wrapped around her shoulders.

Everyone was dressed in his or her Christmas best and once again with the help of Sara and Willie, Nate and I looked pretty good. Well, Nate sure did. I kept sneaking peeks at him as the "city girls" took notice and flocked around him. Erg. Nate seemed to enjoy the attention, which just made me madder. I told myself to get a grip and forced a calm ladylike expression on my face.

I spotted Robert scanning the room with his eyes, looking pleased at what he saw. He stopped when his gaze came to me, and then walked confidently across the floor to my side. "Could I have the pleasure of this dance?"

"I'd be delighted," I said, glancing in Nate's direction, hoping he'd notice that even though all the young men weren't lining up to ask me to dance, I wasn't a dishcloth either. Robert noticed me. And as uncomfortable as he made me feel, his company was still better than reverting to the wallflower I usually was.

"Cassandra, you look lovely as usual," Robert cooed. Well, maybe he didn't coo. Really, I didn't get his fascination with me. I wasn't rich, or any prettier than a lot of the girls in the room or even consistent. Here today, gone tomorrow.

"Thank you."

We swirled around the dance floor and it pleased me to see Nate staring with a disgruntled expression.

"Your brother doesn't like me." So, Robert noticed it, too.

"Who cares what my brother thinks."

"You are so intriguing!" he spouted. Why? Because I didn't care what my "brother" thought? I didn't know what to say so I just smiled.

"You are spirited, spontaneous, and unpredictable. I like that in a woman."

Diversion! Diversion!

"You know, I was with Sara when she delivered her baby brother. No midwife or anything." Robert grimaced slightly. I could tell I was going in the wrong direction with this but couldn't stop now. "I almost fainted but Sara was amazing. Practically Wonder Woman."

"Wonder woman?" His eyes sparkled with amusement. "Cassandra, you say the most provocative things."

Brother. Okay, I got it. Robert Willingsworth was into me. What should I do about it? There was nothing I could do until this really long dance ended. I decided the best tactic was to change the subject.

"Those are lovely, large portraits on the wall. Family?"

"Indeed. My father, grandfather and great grandfather." He motioned to the three prominent paintings that hung in a row on the far wall. "All plantation men."

"What do you mean?"

"I'm originally from the south. I've mentioned that before, I believe."

"Yes, I remember. Is that how your family made their fortune, off the plantations?"

"Cotton is very profitable."

"Then why did you move to Boston?"

"Factories. New technology makes the spinning of cotton thread much faster and more profitable. My father came to Boston to open a clothing factory and that's when I decided to follow him and attend Harvard. Now I oversee operations."

"You once mentioned that it was the success of these very factories that increased the need for slave labor in the south. Do you support this, Robert?"

"And as I expected, Cassandra, you are also very intelligent. But, please, this is too festive of an occasion for such serious talk. Let's save politics for another time, shall we."

The music ended and I curtsied to excuse myself. "I think, I'll go, and uh, get a drink of punch." I turned, hoping to leave Robert behind, but he followed me.

"Allow me to assist you." Like I couldn't get my own drink? While Robert poured my punch I scanned the room for Nate, fully expecting him to be dancing with some pretty girl. Instead he was standing against the wall glaring at me.

Robert handed me a glass cup with a tiny little glass handle. I took it carefully, not wanting to spill on Sara's dress. "Thank you,

Robert." He seemed to be waiting for approval. I took a sip. "Um, it's lovely."

"Great. I'm glad you like it."

Okay. Now what? "Um, I'm going to go speak with my brother."

"I'll accompany you."

Was he kidding me? Was he my shadow now?

"You know, Robert, actually, I need to visit the powder room."

That stumped him. "Of course, I'll have my man, George, show you the way."

He waved his man over and I followed him, breathing a sigh of relief. I took a moment to powder my nose and tuck a flyaway curl behind my ear. Robert Willingsworth was suffocating me. Funny how I'd rather spend a quiet evening in the cabin talking to Nate, than be at this fancy ball with Robert.

Soon after I rejoined the party, Robert's domestic help made an announcement that dinner was served. I didn't even know there was going to be a dinner. Wasn't this amazing dance enough? How much did it cost to feed all these people? We were ushered into an adjoining room filled with round tables, fully loaded with expensive looking dinnerware and candelabras. Robert had arranged the seating so that he would be next to me. Nate and Sara and Willie sat across from us. Both Nate and Sara seemed to be in sour moods. The food was delicious, and that cheered Nate up a bit. Roast duck with some kind of orange sauce, mashed potatoes, cranberries, rolls, sparkling wine and apple juice and more sweets than you could count.

"I love a woman with a good appetite," Robert said to me.

Oh. Was I making a pig of myself? Should I eat slower? The conversations at all the tables in the vast room created a loud din, making it hard to talk quietly. Robert shouted across the table to Nate, Sara and Willie, "Are you having a good time?"

Thankfully, Willie answered for them. "Yes, very nice. Thank you again for inviting us to your Christmas party. It's very generous of you to include our whole family."

"It is my pleasure." He addressed Nate. "I hope you don't mind my dominating your sister's time tonight. You can't blame a man for desiring the company of such a beautiful woman."

Did he really say that? Out loud? Well, he hasn't seen my knobby knees. But the better question was, why didn't Nate think I was beautiful? Not that I was. Just saying. Of course, Robert had never met Jessica Fuller. I wondered if he'd still want me if she were in the room. Nate seemed at a loss for words. Did he mind or didn't he? He started choking on something then, and took a swig of water. He never answered Robert's question.

Robert kept talking. "I wish that your father was here, Cassandra."

"Why?" What did my dad have to do with anything?

"Because, I am the type of man who likes to do things properly. I would like to ask your father for your hand in marriage."

What! Both Nate and Sara blanched as white as the crisply starched tablecloth. Willie seemed equally stunned. No one saw that coming.

"Robert, we barely know each other," I managed to cough up.

"I know everything I need to know. I haven't stopped thinking about you since the day we met in the bookstore. You are what I want, and I don't mean to sound conceited, but I always get what I want."

Nate's hands clasped the top of the table, his knuckles white. I pleaded with my eyes, help me!

"Uh, Robert," Nate said, "since our father isn't present, I must speak as the man of the house, uh, male responsible for Case, uh, Cassandra, and I think she's too young."

"With all due respect, Nathaniel, Cassandra is a woman of marrying age. I am a man in good standing and of substantial means. I would take excellent care of her and your family, too. Our union would be mutually beneficial."

Our union? Ew, gross. Sara went from white to red to white again. I hated that I was playing a part in her heartache.

"Cassandra darling," Robert said, "I would like to hear from you. May I speak with your father to ask for his permission for us to marry?"

My head filled with buzzing. My eyes darted to each face at my table, Willie, Sara, Nate, all with frozen expressions of shock. I swiveled slightly to take in the rest of the room. Was it my imagination or had the dining hall grown quiet? Yes, it had. Very quiet, indeed.

FIFTEEN

I DIDN'T KNOW WHY he got so mad. What did he care, really? When we were finally alone in our cabin, Nate snapped, "What were you thinking?"

"It's not like I said yes."

Nate paced our small room raking his hand through his hair, short little puffing snorts coming through his nose.

"Everyone was looking at me. The whole room just got quiet, I mean, what was that about? And I didn't say yes." Who did Nate think he was anyway? "I said maybe. How can that be considered a yes?"

"Because," Nate said slowly as if he were talking to a child, "maybe isn't NO."

"I couldn't very well come right out and say that, could I?" I splashed water onto my face and brushed my teeth with my finger. "I mean, he's Robert Willingsworth, rich guy, lots of friends and a Very Important Person. It would have been inconsiderate of me to embarrass him after he'd been so generous inviting everyone to his mansion."

"So he's a VIP, but what about Sara Watson? Anyone can see she's crazy about him."

"That's obvious to everyone except Robert." Or maybe not. He probably knew he would hurt her by proposing to me in her presence. What a jerky thing to do. "Why do you think he would propose to me with a room full of people watching?" I stomped across to my side of the cabin. "He was trying to manipulate me into saying yes, can't you see that?"

Behind the sheet I let my dress drop to the floor and scurried under my covers. "More than anything I hate how this hurts Sara, but I don't think humiliating her family in front of all of Boston would've helped."

Nate carried the candle to the small table between our beds. He sat up with his back against the wall, a position that gave him full view of my side of the room through the crack between the wall and the hanging sheet. I needed to fix that, pronto. My own blanket was pulled up to my chin, but still. He made me nervous with the way he was staring. He was so intense. I knew he was mad I had hurt Sara and by extension the Watson family. I mean, the ride home in the carriage had been chilly—not just the cold weather kind—and having Robert kiss my hand as he helped me into the carriage hadn't helped.

I blew out the candle; the sudden darkness removed me from Nate's strange staring behavior. I turned to the wall and pretended to sleep. What more could I say? The whole situation was just so bizarre. Sharing a room with Nate was getting really uncomfortable, even if he was just supposed to be my brother.

The next morning I met Sara in the kitchen. She mumbled "Good Morning" without looking me in the eyes. She stood at the sink with her shoulders hunched, keeping her back to me.

"Sara," I started.

"No need to say anything. It's clear to me the way things stand." She dropped a loaf of bread on the cutting board and started sawing it into slices as if to save her life. "I'm very happy for you." She didn't sound happy for me.

"Sara, please. I don't even want to marry Robert." She stopped sawing.

"He put me in a very awkward position. My choices were to let him hear what he wanted to hear, or embarrass him in front of everyone."

Sara put the knife down and turned to me. Her eyes were red from crying. "I'm sorry. It's not your fault that Robert loves you and not me. It was wrong of me to be angry."

I was almost certain that Robert loved Robert and not me or Sara, but I didn't say that. Sara reached for a wrapped package on the table. "These came for you this morning."

"From...?" I was sick of saying his name. Sara nodded. I opened it without ceremony. It was a box of chocolates.

"Nice," Sara said graciously. "Those are from the finest chocolatier in Boston." Removing the lid, I offered the open box to Sara.

"Take one."

"No, I'm fine."

"Are you sure?" I plopped a piece into my mouth. "Umm. This is so good! Come on. You have to have one."

She smiled, relenting. Nothing so girlfriend bonding as a good box of chocolates. "Okay," Sara said, after finishing her third piece. "What are you going to do about Robert? He thinks you agreed to marry him."

"I'm going to have to tell him I'm not."

"How do you plan to do that?"

"I guess I'll just go to his house." She raised her eyebrows.

"Just go to his house? Cassandra, you can't just show up at Robert's house uninvited. Especially, not alone."

"Why not?"

She sputtered for a moment. "It's just not done!"

"Oh." I popped a caramel filled piece of chocolate. "Ten, I hab to tink of some-ting elf."

Sara burst out laughing.

The door knocker sounded and she was still giggling when she called for Missy to answer the door. Missy returned.

"It's Mr. Willingsworth for Miss Cassandra."

My mouth was full of chocolate! My hair, a rat's nest. I was so not expecting company. Sara saw my startled look, handed me a glass of water and a bonnet that hung on a hook by the back door.

"Oh my goodness, Sara! He's here. What am I going to do?"

"Tell him the truth."

Right. The truth. I stood and smoothed out my skirt. Ugh. Well, this was guaranteed to be a very unpleasant experience; might as well get it over with.

"This shouldn't take long."

Robert was taken aback by my unruly appearance (though, it might work in my favor), but recovered quickly. "Cassandra, darling." He took two long strides to reach me, placing his hands gently on my shoulders. "My apologies, my dear. I should have sent a messenger to let you know I was coming."

"Actually, I'm glad you came. We need to talk."

"Indeed we do. Shall we sit down?"

We sat in the living room in front of the fireplace. Sara shooed away the kids that were playing hide and seek and then slipped discreetly into the kitchen.

"Now, obviously, Cassandra," Robert began, "I am disappointed that you didn't give me a clear and positive response last night, especially in front of my guests, but I will take the blame for that. I shouldn't have surprised you with such an important question in public."

Robert shifted off the chair. Oh no, he was getting down on one knee!

"Cassandra, darling, marry me." It didn't sound like a question. More like a command, with his expectation certain that after a good night's sleep, I would have come to my senses.

"Robert, I can't marry you."

His eyelashes fluttered involuntarily, "What?"

"I'm sorry. I didn't mean to lead you on in any way."

"Lead me on?"

"I was only trying to be your friend."

"My friend?"

Was he just going to keep repeating me? "Yes, I want to be your friend, but I'm not ready to get married."

He huffed, smirked and then he started belly laughing. This guy was whacked.

"Oh, Cassandra, you are so funny. Of course you are ready to get married. All girls your age are dying to get married. Now, I understand if the idea of us, uh, being intimate..."

"Oh, I so didn't need that mental picture. "...makes you a little nervous, well, that's normal." He put his hand on my knee and smiled. "I promise that you will enjoy our wedding night."

I stood up sharply. Robert's hand dropped to his lap. "That's not what I meant."

"Perhaps I am still rushing things." Robert stood, tugging on his lapels. "I will return tomorrow and we can speak of this again."

"No. Not tomorrow, Robert. Please, don't make this any harder than it has to be."

Robert's lips twitched. "I know what this is about."

Besides the fact that he was so not my type? Not to mention from the wrong century?

"Cobbs has talked to you," he said.

"What? How do you know Cobbs?" Tiny nervous shivers crept up my arms as the clues started to fall into place. "Is that why you saw us at the tavern? You were with Cobbs?" He didn't deny it. I was flabbergasted. "You capture runaway slaves for reward?"

"The reward is just peanuts to me. It's the principle of the thing. Had I known you had returned once again to the Watsons', I wouldn't have employed Cobbs. There are plenty like him who'd jump at the chance to work for me. Besides, he is a rather unreliable type of fellow. It's probably all for the best." He didn't seem at all worried about how I might feel about this. Surely, he must have heard from Cobbs that Nate and I had freed Samuel?

Or maybe he hadn't made the connection before?

"What were you and your brother doing at the tavern that day?"

He knew Samuel got away. Now he knew we had something to do with it. "We were just riding."

"Just riding?"

He paced the living room, a long finger on his chin, "Just riding, you say. Well, tell me, my dear, why do you leave Cambridge all the time? Where do you go?"

He made me sick. "I don't have to answer to you."

"I beg to differ. We are betrothed, if you don't recall. Soon, you will be Mrs. Willingsworth, and you will answer to me."

Was he trying to scare me? "I will not marry you."

Robert grabbed my arm, squeezing it hard. He pulled me close, and not in a romantic way. He was trying to scare me—and it was working.

"I don't know who you think you are, Cassandra Donovan, but no one publicly humiliates me, no one!"

"Ouch, you're hurting me!"

Instead of loosening his grip he pressed tighter, "You don't even know the meaning of pain, my dear. Do you understand me?"

The door from the kitchen burst open. Nate! His gaze moved

from Robert's hand on my arm, to my face. His eyes narrowed. "Is everything all right?"

Robert smiled like a boy caught stealing candy. His fingers uncurled from my arm. I rubbed the spot furiously with my other hand. There would be bruising. Nate stepped in between Robert and me, fire in his eyes. His hands kept curling into fists.

"Ah, the brother," Robert said, "or are you?"

I jumped in, "Of course he is. What are you saying?"

"I'm saying that the mystery I found so attractive in you, involves him somehow. The way he looks at you, it's not natural for a brother."

He pulled his vest down sharply."So, yes, I think you are right after all, my dear. There will be no wedding."

He turned to leave. "Please, I will find my own way out."

Nate's eyes were closed tight in the way that you do when you're trying to control your anger. He breathed in deeply then turned to me.

"Casey, are you okay?" I thought I was. I nodded my head stoically, but my eyes gave me away. I wiped away tears.

"Your timing was amazing."

"Sara came to the barn looking for me. She told me Robert had arrived."

He shifted around uncomfortably. "I thought maybe you'd need moral support, to uh, do the right thing."

The door to the kitchen cracked open. I called quietly, "Sara?"

Sara opened the door wider. "Excuse me, I didn't mean to intrude."

"It's okay. It's over now. He's gone."

"Cassandra, did he hurt you?" She saw me rubbing my arm.

"A bit, but I'm okay."

Sara stared at the carpet, dumbfounded. "I'd never believe him capable of such ungentlemanly behavior."

"I'm just glad we all know the truth now."

Suddenly, I felt tired. "I think I need to lie down for awhile."

"Of course," Sara rushed to my side, ready to usher me out.

"Sara," Nate said, "I'll take her."

"Oh," she said. "Certainly."

Nate put his arms around my shoulders and walked me outside. I felt fussed over. "I'm okay, you know. I could walk myself."

Nate shrugged. He was too busy grinding his teeth to say anything. We were almost at the cabin. I was just happy to be this close to him right now, basically hugging. Two more steps to the cabin. One more step. Dizziness. A flash of light. I grabbed Nate's hand. The food court.

SIXTEEN

"WE'RE BACK," I SAID. We both had dark rings around our eyes, a pair of raccoons. The birthday gift bag still sat on the table, empty hot fudge containers beside it. Tyson and Josh still ate burgers, oblivious to us. And Lucinda sat wide-eyed and open-mouthed. Probably because my hair was a wild mess when just seconds ago, her seconds, it'd been pulled back nicely in a pony-tail; and also because Nate still had his arm around me.

Oh, yeah, and Jessica was still coming up the escalator, in full view of her boyfriend apparently snuggling with her nemesis. Me. First, she screamed. Not a "there's a hair in my soup" scream, but a "Freddy Krueger is coming after me with his claws" scream. Everyone—the cashier at the Chubby Chicken outlet, the geek teens in line at New York fries, a couple of senior citizens ordering Big Macs—stopped what they were doing to watch and listen. The only sound in the food court besides the piped in Christmas music was the wail of a toddler who just dropped her ice cream cone when her startled mother flinched.

"Oh boy," Nate said.

"Nate! What are you doing?!" Her strawberry blond hair

flung out of place with the whipping of her head as she stormed over to our table. By then Nate had removed the offending arm and scuttled a few inches away from me.

"Hi, Jessica," he said. She dismissed his greeting.

"Why are you sitting with her? Why did you have your arm around her?"

Nate stood and rubbed his eyes. I rubbed mine too, just because. Kind of like contagious yawning.

"Jessica," he said wearily, "don't make a big deal of it. I was just wishing Casey a happy birthday."

"So? Why would you care? She's so, so..."

So, what? So beneath him?

"Jess, please, just drop it." She softened, smart enough (barely) to see that her tantrum wasn't working. She reached her hand out to him. He seemed reluctant to take it, but did. She pulled him along, pressing up close to him. She said loud enough for everyone to hear, "Babe, please promise me you will never go near her again."

Nate glanced at me, his expression tight, then back to Jessica. "No, I won't promise that." Yeah! My heart skipped around like a little kid in the playground. He had stood up to his evil girlfriend.

"Why not? What's she to you?"

Nate hunched over and hushed her. "Leave it alone, okay? We can talk about it later."

"Why can't we talk about it now? You don't like her, do you?" I felt embarrassed for him. It was like trying to reason with a drunk. And I was interested in his answer.

"Baby?" she persisted. Then, as if she actually saw him now, instead of the drama. "You look awful, Nate. What's wrong with you?"

"Jessica, I didn't want to do this here, but I can't take it anymore. I want out."

"What?"

"It's not working."

"What's not working?"

"Us."

"Us?"

Nate nodded.

"You're breaking up with me?"

"Yes."

Wow. Double wow.

By now, Tyson and Josh had strolled over. Tyson sipped soda from a straw, which couldn't have been easy since he had a big grin on his face. I would guess that Tyson didn't like Jessica that much either. Jessica pushed Nate away with two hands against his chest. Then she shook her long fake fingernail at me.

"You! I don't know how you did this, you frizzy-haired, plain-faced freak, but I will not forget it."

Okay, I could have lived without the body image slams in front of Nate, and well, in front of the whole food court. Nate walked away with his friends, catching my eye first and offering me a soft salute as he left. I could hear Tyson saying, "Dude! What was that all about?"

Lucinda leaned in close. "He just tripped with you? Again?"

I nodded and sighed. "Why do you keep doing that?" The way her lips tightened in a line I could tell she was mad. I didn't get that.

"I didn't do it. He touched me."

She leaned back and crossed her arms. "You need to be more careful. Wear gloves."

Wear gloves? Twenty-four seven?

She persisted. "So, what happened this time? Why did he have his arm around you?"

I didn't like her tone. "What is this, the inquisition?"

"Casey, it's just that it's what, twice, in how many weeks?

You need to be more responsible. What if something happened to him?"

Fatigue weighed on me and I really just wanted to go home to bed. "Can we have this conversation later?"

"Okay, fine." She picked up her coat and purse. "But, tomorrow after you've slept this off, you are telling me ev-er-ree-thing."

"Deal." I leaned against her as we rode the elevator down, exhausted.

SOMEONE SHOOK MY SHOULDER. "Sweetheart? You've been sleeping for a long time. Are you feeling okay?"

"Mom?" Waking up in a new time era was always a bit discombobulating. I was used to waking at the crack of dawn in the freezing cold, watching Nate struggle to make the fire. Now I snuggled underneath my steel blue bedspread, spacing out.

"What day is it?" I asked.

"It's Sunday, just after three o'clock. You've been sleeping for almost twenty-four hours."

"Oh," I rubbed my dry, gritty eyes. "Well, you know how teenagers can sleep."

Mom sat on the side of my bed and studied me. "You'd win a gold medal in the sleep event, honey." My mother had soft wrinkles around her eyes and mouth that I thought only added to her prettiness. I reached for her arm and surprised myself with an unfamiliar wave of affection. I realized that I'd missed her.

I'd been tempted to tell her about my other life many times. But really, what would a parent do if their kid told them a wild story like that? Spend tons of money on a shrink for kids, that's what. I'd have to take her back to prove it, and after what I just went through with Nate, well, I was convinced that would be a bad idea. What if something happened to her there? This knowledge and her helplessness to protect me would just send her over a cliff with worry.

She let go of my hand and stood. "You should get up now. You have school tomorrow and you won't be able to sleep tonight at this rate."

"I'll be right down. I'm starving." I settled for a quick bowl of cereal to tide me over to dinner and snuggled into my usual spot on the sofa in the living room. Mom was there, watching one of her home makeover shows. "Where's Tim?" I said, wiping milk off my chin.

Mom breathed in deeply, "In his room."

Oh, right. Tim's police escort and etc.

"And Dad?" I added hopefully.

"He's gone." She said this without the usual heaviness attached to her voice. In fact, I'd swear I'd seen a slight, though brief, grin.

"How are things going, you know, with you and Dad?" I ventured. Then I realized my birthday here was only yesterday.

"Oh, Casey," Mom shrugged, answering anyway. "I don't know. It's complicated." Complicated isn't the same as over. I had hope.

"When's he coming again?"

"He's coming back in a few days to talk to Tim. Tim just won't listen to me. Part of his grounding is no computer video games, just homework, but I know he's upstairs playing that stupid war game." At least Tim's antics were bringing Dad home more often.

WE HAD one week of school before the Christmas break. I couldn't remember if I had homework, so I went back upstairs to check my bag, stopping at Tim's room on my way. Even though he'd just seen me yesterday morning, it'd been over two weeks since I'd seen him. In a weird way I'd missed him, too.

"Hey," I said.

"What d' you want?"

"Nothing. Just dropped in to say 'hi'."

He looked at me with suspicion.

"Did Mom send you to check on me? Tell her I'm doing my homework." Except that he wasn't. He was playing the war game.

"You're stressing Mom out."

"I'm not doing anything to her." Tim's eyes stayed glued to his monitor screen.

"You're not doing what she said."

"So. Who are you, the parental police?"

"It's hard for her with Dad gone."

"Their problems are not my problems. Now, do you mind?" Tim swiveled in his chair impatiently.

"Okay, fine."

"Whatever." What an immature little twit! If he wasn't bigger than me, I'd smack him. I returned to my room and dragged my backpack onto my bed. I dug out my planner and reviewed my homework. Algebra and Biology. Better get this done and out of the way. Who knew what tomorrow would bring.

My locker Monday morning had been tagged. In lipstick. A loopy, greasy red smudge said, *Loser*. I scrubbed it with a tissue. It must have been a cheap brand (or maybe an expensive brand—I wasn't a lipstick girl), because the waxy lip color refused to come off.

The tag stubbornly stuck. I just about had the faint shadow of the big flouncy "L" erased when someone eased up to the locker next to me.

I couldn't contain my surprise. Nate had his shoulder pressed against the locker, his arms confidently crossed. I opened my locker door wide. I didn't want him to know Jessica had left her mark.

"What are you doing here?" I'd fully expected a return to the let's pretend we don't know each other game we usually played. It looked like Nate was prepared to bend the rules.

"Is that how you say 'hello', these days?"

He cleaned up nice; smelled so musky good. I grabbed a textbook.

"Hello." I noted he kept a safe distance. I should wear a neon T-shirt that says, Careful, Don't Touch.

He looked directly at me, staring again. "I just wanted to make sure you were okay."

What did he mean? Okay, because I'd nearly been engaged to an abuser, or okay that I'd witnessed his breakup with Evil Girl-friend, or okay that I'd gotten a good sleep?

"I'm fine. And you?"

He smiled, "Yeah, I'm cool."

"Good."

"Well, I just thought I'd say 'hello', so see you around."

No sense in overdoing it. I nodded my head as he left. "Yeah, see you."

After spending the last two days looking like a fashion wreck in need of a shower, I'd spent a little more effort than usual on my appearance. Yes, Jessica's words had stung, and yes, I did care what Nate thought, but it was also time for me to care about myself. I'd washed my hair with strawberry shampoo and condi-tioner, and plastered in lots of mousse and gel so my curls were tamer than usual; I wore a bit of mascara and lip-gloss, added a touch of color to my pale cheeks. I wore my best jeans and the graphic long sleeve T-shirt Lucinda had bought me. Maybe that was why Nate had stopped to stare? Lucinda noticed, too.

"Wow, you look great, Case. I knew that shirt would look terrific on you. A good night's sleep totally did wonders." Then she furrowed her brow. "This metamorphosis wouldn't have anything to do with a certain athlete in the school?"

"Metamorphosis? Was I that bad?"

"No, you're fine. So, tell me about your little vacation."

She was acting so strange and pushy about this; I found I didn't want to tell her.

"Nothing really. You've been there. Boring, actually."

"So, no romance this time around?"

I stabbed her with a glare. "Believe me, if Nate and I'd hooked up, you'd be the first to know."

We ate lunch in the cafeteria in our usual places with an easy view of the jock table. I tried really hard not to look at Nate because every time I did, Lucinda would stare at me suspiciously, like she'd caught me in a lie.

Nate didn't seem to have the same problem. He openly looked my way and smiled.

"He seems to like you," Lucinda commented loudly. "He can't seem to keep his eyes away."

"Keep your voice down, Luce. What's the matter with you?"

"Hey, you know everything about me. I'm not the one keeping secrets here."

She stood up. "Look, I got to go. I'll see you after last class."

So, I was dismissed. My best friend had just dismissed me. I scraped my tray, sneaking glimpses Nate's way. A new girl was sitting at his table on the opposite side of Nate, beside Tyson. I recognized her from my Algebra class; the teacher had called her Kelly. She was pale and petite and blond, a stark contrast to Tyson's height and athleticism and dark skin. I was kind of jealous that she sat at the same table as Nate, but by the way she was flirting with Tyson, I didn't think I had to worry.

My next class was English. Last time we'd returned from tripping, Nate had thoroughly ignored me. His friendliness earlier today led me to believe he would be less frosty than before.

"Okay, class, listen up," Mr. Turner said. "Your assignment for this week is to write a Shakespearean type play of your own." A loud groan went up from the class.

"Just three acts, a minimum of twelve pages. And, you can do it with a partner if you want." Really? A partner? I couldn't help but look to Nate. As usual, my view was the back of his head. So maybe I was wrong? Then he swiveled around, caught my eyes and mouthed, "You and me?"

Yes! In more ways than one. Shock muted me, so I just nodded. We rearranged our desks so that we sat beside each other. Nate smiled, still keeping a safe distance.

"So, what should we write about?" I said, working hard at controlling the quiver in my voice. "Any ideas?"

He put his finger to his nose, feigning deep thought. "Well, we could write about a girl who travels spontaneously to the past and gets into all kinds of trouble there." The corner of his lips tugged upwards. "I don't think that's been done."

"Hmm, it could work. Mystery, intrigue, a villain." I thought of Robert dressed in tights and a jester's hat.

"Don't forget the dashing love interest."

Gulp.

How could I forget that? The question was, do they get together in the end?

AFTER SCHOOL, I met up with Lucinda at the gym. The senior varsity boys' basketball team was already hard at practicing lay-ups and foul shots, and the echoes of a dozen balls reverberated through the gym. Lucinda popped a stick of gum in her mouth and offered me some.

"Thanks," I said. As I chewed, my eyes scanned the team for Nate. He saw me walk in and nodded in acknowledgment. Nate glistened with sweat, his muscles flexing as he made another shot.

He was so hot! Oh, help me. Being friends with Nate might prove to be harder than being ignored by him. Lucinda witnessed our interaction.

"I really do think he's into you," she said, sounding baffled. Did she have to seem so surprised by the possibility? Geez.

"Okay, hypothetically, what if he was?"

"It's just that no one has ever seen the two of you together. Ever. Well, outside of your English class, which doesn't really count. I mean, you guys travel in different universes."

"We're not different species."

"No." Lucinda stared at the cheerleaders—led by Jessica—all high fashion, faces perfectly and heavily made up, hair iron-straightened, not a curl in sight. "But almost. Casey, it's not like you're ugly or anything."

"Thanks, Lucinda."

"Don't take it the wrong way. Anyone with eyes can see you were born beautiful. You are really defensive today, though."

The new girl, Kelly, tentatively peeked in through the gym doors. We'd had Algebra together earlier. I waved her over.

"Hey," she said, and then I introduced her to Lucinda. Kelly seemed comfortable with us. I saw her eye the cheerleaders, but she didn't seem inclined to join them. For that reason, I liked her. Nate passed the ball to Tyson, who made an easy basket.

"He's good," I said. It was a test to see how she'd respond.

"I know," Kelly swooned.

"You're so gone for him!"

"Can you tell?" She looked sincerely concerned.

Lucinda piped up. "Well, yeah."

"How do you know him?" I asked.

"Our dads went to college together. When my father was transferred to New England his company let him choose where he wanted to live. He chose Cambridge so he 'could go for a beer' with Tyson's dad," she said using finger quotes.

"Does Tyson know how you feel?"

"I don't know. He probably just sees us as friends. You can't say anything, okay?" Kelly's face pinched with worry.

"It's okay," I assured her. "Your secret is safe with us. But you might not want to keep it a secret from him."

Tyson glanced our way. I was certain his eyes remained on Kelly a second longer than they would have for just a friend. "I think he likes you, too."

"Really?" Kelly said, nervously pulling at her short pixie-like golden hair.

"Yes, really." I had to leave without saying good-bye to Nate, which shouldn't have bothered me, but it did. Maybe I was making too much of his friendliness today. Just because he was nice today didn't mean he wanted more than friendship from me. He's a nice guy. He was just being nice. Nice, nice, nice.

SEVENTEEN

DAD CAME FOR DINNER on Christmas day bringing us all gifts, even one for Mom. She fussed about how they had agreed not to exchange gifts, though she seemed truly pleased with the colorful framed painting that Dad bought her.

"I was thinking of painting the living room again with these exact colors," she said, propping it up against the living room wall. Good, she was thinking about painting our walls again. A sure sign she was recovering from her slump.

I had knitted Tim a scarf. Yes, I know. Maybe because he had ticked me off so much recently. An interesting yellow/green color.

"It looks like barf," he said.

"Tim!" my mother reprimanded. "She worked hard to make you that. Now say thank you to your sister."

"Thanks for the barf scarf, sis."

Nate and his parents went to Canada for Christmas when they found out his brother would be home on leave from Afghanistan for a few days. After seeing so much of Nate lately, it was weird to know he wasn't around. I'd been watching for him on Facebook ever since he'd left. A lot. Kind of stalker-like. I checked his status to make sure he'd changed it from "in a relationship" to "single" which he had. Good. Finally, on the third day, I scrolled halfway down the page and there it was. His name. My heart did a little dance. His profile picture had been updated. The latest photo was of Nate and his brother, arms around each other, both with big grins.

Nate Mackenzie is happy to see his brother, home from Afghanistan for the holidays.

I pressed 'comment' and a little window opened up, next to my profile picture which was mostly hair. The cursor flashed, waiting for me to type something. What to say? I typed:

Casey Donovan How's Toronto? Say 'hi' to John for me. Was that too weird? Too familiar? I'd never even met John. I cleared it and changed it to:

Casey Donovan So cool you can see your brother again.

Holding my breath, I clicked the comment button. I stared at the screen, willing for a reply. Amazingly, it worked. His name popped up in the chat box at the bottom of the screen.

Hi C. Toronto's cold. Yeah, John's cool.

I quickly typed in:

Cold here too. Not the same with you gone.

I pressed enter without thinking. Oops. Did that sound too mushy? Pushy? Oh, no. Needy? Ugh. Why did I write that? Wait for a reply. Wait. Wait. Nothing. Maybe he had to go. Unlike me, he probably had lots to do, hanging with his brother and all. I re-read my comment. Not the same without you. That wasn't so bad. Was it? I'd say something like that to Lucinda, wouldn't I? Sure. I tried to comfort myself. It was a completely harmless comment. Then suddenly, his response:

Are you staying put?

A surge of glee coursed through me. He wanted to know if I'd traveled since the last time. He was checking up on me.

So far. Kind of boring though.

He sent back.

Boring is good for you C, for a change. See you in January.

I spent New Year's at Lucinda's for our annual, current-celebrity movie/TV series-sleepover marathon. We'd done this together every year since eighth grade, because neither of us ever got invited to the cool parties. Previous years had featured Zac Efron, Orlando Bloom, Robert Pattison and Brad Pitt (even though he's kind of old, he's still, well, wow).

We didn't talk about Nate, or tripping or her jealous/weird behavior. We kept the conversation to safe topics like celebrity crushes, and her sisters' ongoing relational dramas.

When school resumed in January, I tried desperately to keep my cool. I challenged myself not to scan the hallways for his face or think about him for every second of the day. However, I couldn't avoid English (surprising how it jumped back to being my favorite class), and we had to finish our project.

We met up in the library. Seeing him again was harder than I'd thought because, despite—or maybe because of—everything we'd been through together, he still made me nervous.

"Did you have a nice Christmas?" he said politely. I nodded. He sat beside me but leaned back. I'm no body language expert, but I didn't think that boded well in my favor. He acted so stiff, you'd think we'd never had that Facebook connection.

"You?"

"Yeah, lot of family stuff. Also visited York University."

My eyebrows shot up. "Why's that?"

"I've been offered a full scholarship."

My throat suddenly dried out. I choked, "At York? In Toronto?"

He clicked his pen. "Yup."

"Oh, wow. That's great." That's terrible! I forced a smile. "You must be excited."

"I'm relieved. It's nice to finally know what I'm going to do after grad."

He might be relieved, but I was having a sudden panic attack.

"What about you?"

"Huh?"

"What about you? You must have plans for after you graduate."

"Oh, yeah, sure, well, I still have a couple years to decide. And it's not like I could do just any job." I was grasping. "I couldn't be a pilot like your dad, for instance."

"True. You need to do something that doesn't require constant mental awareness."

"So brain surgery is out?"

"I would say so. But you could be a writer, or computer tech or a number of other things that wouldn't endanger your life or the lives of others, when...."

Yeah, when I trip off to the nineteenth century.

A knot of anger had formed in my gut. "You're right, Nate. I should be thinking about how I'm going to keep a roof over my head when I'm not, you know, busy with other things."

It wasn't fair to feel this way toward Nate. I couldn't expect him to hang around for me. And he was right. I couldn't live with my mom forever, either.

"So, let's get this done," I said through gritted teeth. He might have been relieved to let me know he had plans. I was relieved to finish this dumb project so I wouldn't have to sit so painfully close to him ever again. I wasn't that great at hiding my feelings.

"Casey, I know I upset you."

I faked a scoff. "I'm not upset."

"I think I know you pretty well. I can tell you're upset."

He knows me pretty well? He's right, he does know me! My face flushed and I pushed down the urge to bawl like a baby.

"Every time I see you," he said, "the first thing I look for are rings under your eyes."

What, wait a minute. Really? "So?"

"So, I care about you. I worry..." He worries? He cares? Except, what about York University? How does that fit in? How could he care about me from CANADA? How long before "out of sight, out of mind" kicks in? I shook my head. It wouldn't work.

"That means a lot, Nate. Thanks. But I have my whole life ahead of me, and I'm sure I'll manage on my own."

I pushed away from the table. His pen rolled onto the floor.

I leaned to pick it up. He did too. Our eyes connected, just like the first time we met and I could see the little freckle under his eye. My hand still reached for the floor. So did his. He missed his pen and grabbed my hand. My heart raced. And we tumbled towards the light. In one disconcerting moment, the library and all the shelves of books disappeared. The school, parking lot, students all gone.

"Oh no," I said, gently pulling away. Why was I tripping so much lately? I stared at Nate. He was the problem. He caused my heart to gear into overdrive and thrust us into the past. "I'm sorry," I said. Though it was his fault.

"It's okay. It's not like you can help it." He smiled. "I guess I'll have to work harder at keeping my hands off you."

Wow. I could not read this guy. Did he like me or not? And if he did like me and he didn't mind an occasional time travel trip, why was he planning to move to Toronto? I collected my thoughts.

"We should go back to the Watsons'."

"Do you think they'd take us in again? We keep leaving without warning."

"I know, but they're kind hearted and forgiving. Besides, I like them. Sara and Willie are my only friends here."

"Don't forget Robert Willingsworth," he said with a smirk.

I punched him in the arm. "Not funny."

"Let's get going then, if we want to make it there before dark."

We walked in the middle of the road, until we heard the horses. Nate clasped my hand and pulled me into the ditch behind the cover of the thick new spring growth. Six men rode by dressed in the blue uniforms of the Union soldier. I held my breath, waiting in silence until they were out of sight.

"It's 1861," I whispered. "The civil war is beginning. Things could get dangerous." We tracked back out of the bush. "I don't remember when the draft started," I added, "but we don't want you getting suited up and sent south."

"Uh, I couldn't agree more," Nate said with a sudden serious-ness. Was he second-guessing his willingness to come back with me? We cut through the forest to get to the Watson farm from the back, hoping not to be spotted until we could find a change of clothes. The cabin appeared secluded, and we managed to creep in undetected. To my relief, a dress remained hanging in the wardrobe. The sheet still hung in the middle, dividing the room in two. I held the dress to my chest, feeling very self-conscious with Nate in the room. Every time we came back, it was like starting over. Nate politely excused himself and went outside, taking a pair of trousers and a work shirt with him. He tapped on the door before coming back in.

"Are you ready?" he said. I spread the skirt of my dress wide and twirled around.

"How do I look?"

"Exquisite, as per usual." The way his eyes lit up, I believed he meant it.

I was prepared for a lecture from Sara. Bewilderment from Willie. Indifference from the rest of the Watson clan. What I wasn't prepared for were the tears and wailing. It had nothing to do with us. In fact the ripple our appearance caused was barely acknowledged. The whole family surrounded Willie. He was handsomely dressed in a blue Union soldier uniform. He was going south to fight in the war.

"Oh no!" I shocked them all with my outburst. I couldn't stop the tears. I knew what would happen. Over six hundred thousand Americans would lose their lives and many more would return maimed and emotionally scarred.

"Willie? Are you sure? It's really, really, really dangerous."

I tried not to get involved. I'd committed to leaving history to play itself out without my intrusion. But, Willie? I knew him. I liked him. He was my friend.

"It's my duty to my country, Cassandra."

I startled the room—Sara, Mr. and Mrs. Watson and Nate—by throwing my arms around Willie and bursting into tears. "Be safe, Willie, please."

"I'll t-try," he stammered. He hugged me back. "I promise, I'll try."

I stepped back then, wiping my nose in a very unladylike manner, to let the family say proper goodbyes.

"We're praying for you, son," Mr. Watson said, his eyes rimmed red, his normal jovial demeanor heavily subdued. Mrs. Watson cried without restraint, holding Willie tight. "God be with you, son." Sara and all the rest of the Watson kids clamored at his legs. I felt like an intruder in a private moment.

Nate and I slipped out the back.

"I think I'll just go use the restroom," I said, not looking at him. Nothing so not attractive as bloodshot eyes and a matching red nose.

"Sure, I'll meet you back at the cabin." He walked off and I went to the water pump to wash my hands and face.

Samuel was there. "Miss Cassandra?" he said, as surprised as I was. "Are you all right?" I could feel the puffiness in my face.

"Yes, I'm fine." I pushed the handle until water rushed out, then splashed it on my face. "Willie's going to fight in the war. It's terrible. I'm so scared for him."

"It is terrible. I'm sorry to hear it."

"What are you doing here? What happened to you, anyway?"

"Uh, well, I came back hoping to find you. I wanted to thank you again, for rescuing me from Cobbs. That was mighty admirable of you."

Right. That horse chase seemed like ages ago. "I'm sure you would've done the same for me, if our roles were reversed."

"I definitely would have." I don't know what happened next. It remains a blur. I think I fainted, probably a combination of lack of food—I hadn't eaten since breakfast—and emotional overload. Samuel caught me before I hit the ground. I had a sense of his strong arms around me, his handsome face twisted with worry. And then a tunnel of light.

EIGHTEEN

A CACOON OF PURE PANIC encased me. I was certain that I had come home with a stranger from the past and left Nate behind. When the dizziness lifted, I stifled a scream. Instead of the clothes I had on in the library, I still wore my dress from 1861. And I wasn't sitting at the table like I'd expected but standing somewhere outdoors. The biggest mystery though, was what Samuel was wearing. A knitted collared shirt with pencil pants (skinny pant legs, hence the name, but trousers, not jeans) and black loafers on his feet. He looked like Sammy Davis Junior.

With dark circles under his eyes. The expression on his face mirrored mine. "Oh, no," he gulped. That's when I noticed we stood near a street that looked somewhat familiar. The restaurant on the corner with an 'A' frame roofline more common to Switzerland than New England looked brand new. I recognized it now as a car shop off Route 28. In my time the yard was overrun with junkers, and the building looked ready to fall down.

Gawking, I sputtered, "S-s-Samuel?"

Oh, no—Nate! My worst fears had really happened. I'd left Nate behind in the past!

Samuel grabbed my sleeve and tugged me behind an advertising billboard, just as I was about to get bowled over by a boat of a car.

"What was that?" I said.

Samuel said longingly, "A 1959 Chevy Impala hardtop."

That wasn't exactly what I meant, but his answer made me nervous. These massive heavy looking vehicles were everywhere, snaking along the highway, parked in driveways. I had just traveled, I knew that for sure, but now I wasn't sure where I was.

Or rather, when I was?

Suddenly, it made perfect sense. I didn't know if I should be elated or scared to death, but I knew Samuel was like me. I wasn't the only one in the universe.

"Samuel? You're a traveler!" His expression moved from shock to surprise. "That explains a lot," I continued. "Why you showed up and disappeared all the time. Just like me."

Samuel finally found his voice. "You're one, too?"

"Yes, but I'm not from this time. I must have tagged along on your loop."

"My loop?"

"Do you go to the same time era every time?"

"Yes."

"And you come back to your time at the same moment? No one notices that you left?"

"Yes, except for these." He pointed at the darkness under his eyes and then at mine. "It's the same for you," he said wonderingly. We hugged each other for joy, though he pulled away quickly. It just felt so good to find someone else who had to live life with the same oddities and extremes.

"Go home and get dressed!" someone shouted. At me. I looked down at my long dress.

"He must mean me," I said. Samuel nodded.

"Yeah, you look like you're wearing a nightgown." I was just glad I hadn't put a hoop skirt on underneath. I reached up and pulled the bonnet off of my head. I must look like a freak.

"Come," he said, motioning for me to follow. "You need different clothes." I followed, my brain still trying to compute what was going on.

"What year is it by the way?"

"Nineteen sixty-one." Wow. New England had a lot of thick greenness, especially before swaths were cut down for development. This was perfect for dodging out of sight. Samuel led me to a two building apartment complex. The buildings each had three floors and off-white stucco with trim painted aqua blue.

"You should wait here," he said, pointing to a spot behind a garbage dumpster. He strolled across the parking lot dotted with "vintage" cars and lots of children playing hopscotch, skipping rope and jacks. Samuel dodged around them, patting the odd one on the head. All the children were black. In fact, all the inhabitants were black. Mothers calling out the window, kids running in and out, dads coming home from work. There was no way I was going to blend in here.

I peeked around a bit. A red ball rolled by and before I had a chance to duck, a little girl stood almost in front of me. Her face was dark as coffee grounds, with two short black braids sticking out from the sides of her head. Her eyes flicked uncertainly.

"Hi," I said.

"Why are you dressed like that?"

Interesting. She was more taken with my clothes than she was with the color of my skin. I shrugged. "Just for fun. I'm going to change soon."

"Okay." She reached down for her ball and ran off. Samuel pushed through the brush carrying a paper bag.

"Miss Cassandra?"

"You don't have to call me 'Miss' anymore, Samuel." I didn't think it important to go into the little fact that my name was actually Casey.

"Okay. Cassandra." He thrust the bag at me. "Here, it's my sister's."

"Thanks. Uh, where should I change?"

"Oh." He paused for a moment. "I know. Follow me."

Beside the complex bordering green space, was an outbuilding.

"It's a janitor shed," Samuel explained. I stepped inside and shuddered. Obviously the janitor never cleaned this room. I'd disturbed a family of mice, and jumped as they scattered behind mops and pails and sundry items.

The faster I did this the better. I shimmied out of 1861 and put on 1961. What a terrific dress. The fabric was cotton with a feminine blue floral pattern. The bodice fit snugly with the skirt flaring widely at the waist and a hemline that ended just below my knobby knees. A narrow band of matching fabric stretched across my chest and around my shoulders. I loved it.

Samuel also had the foresight to include a pair of shoes. My feet were bigger than his sister's, but thankfully they were open-toed sandals. They also had two-inch pointy heels. I pulled the straps over my ankles and took a tentative step.

He stared at my neck. "Nice cross."

My hand automatically went to my necklace. "Thanks. It's a gift from my dad."

My attention went back to the company in the parking lot. "I noticed that, um, well, I might stand out a bit."

Samuel grunted. "That's an understatement. We have to cross the parking lot to get to the front entrance of my building. Just follow me."

So I did. And I was right. I didn't blend in. Maybe it was the time of day, but all the little kids were suddenly replaced with big ones. Teens. Some playing basketball at one end of the lot; some leaning against cars, or walls, making out.

I heard a whistle. Not a come-to-dinner whistle, but a there's-a-pretty-girl whistle. Or maybe it was a there's-a-white-girl-in-a-black-neighborhood whistle.

"Hey, Samuel," a teen guy shouted. He wore black denim skinny jeans rolled up to his calves just touching the rim of a pair of black boots, and an open bomber jacket with the collar pulled up over a white T-shirt.

"What'ya got there?" He moved in our direction. Three other guys dressed similarly and with poor postures followed behind. A shiver of fear shimmied through my skull.

"Just keep walking," Samuel said stiffly.

"Sam, come on," the leader of the gang said. "We just want to look. We promise we won't touch, right boys?"

"Back off, Jerome!" Samuel snapped. We were almost at the front door, but one of Jerome's posse got there first. I caught hold of Samuel's arm. If stress and tension triggered tripping for him like it did for me, we might be leaving sooner than we thought.

"Is she your girl, Jerome? You Joneses sure like the white ones, don't ya?"

"Just let us get inside. We don't want any trouble."

No, we don't. And I wasn't sure what we could do, outnumbered as we were. If you didn't out-weigh, you had to outwit.

"Hey, boys," I said, winging it. I really had no idea what I was going to do.

"Oooo, she talks," said one.

The next one added, "Aren't you a pretty thing?"

Number three, "When you're done with Sammy boy here, wanna come walk with me?"

If you can't play dead, play stupid. "Oh, could I? I'd love to hang with you boys." I thrust my chest out a bit and pushed a stray strand of hair behind my ear. I wasn't used to flirting, so I probably poured it on a bit too thick. "I just need to use the ladies' room, and then I'll come right out. I promise." I flapped my eyelashes and grinned like a silly hussy. I was crazy to think that would work. Jerome stepped forward, stared deep into my eyes and ran his finger along my jawbone. I worked to keep a flirty face, though my knees were shaking.

Then Jerome said, "Guys, let the doll through."

"Thanks," I said in a husky—and what I hoped was sexy—voice. "See you soon."

We walked casually to the staircase, and I followed Samuel to his first floor apartment. My heart was beating a mile a minute; I felt like a scared rabbit that had just narrowly escaped the claws of the hawk. Soon we were safe. Relatively speaking.

The door to Samuel's home could use a shot of WD40. We were in a small kitchen. The floor had black and white checkerboard tiles, a white fridge shorter than I was, that had rounded corners and a lever for a handle, a small gas stove and a single sink full of dishes. The table was shiny with black and white speckles, chrome trim and legs. At the table sat two wide-eyed little girls about eight and ten years old.

"These are my little sisters, Coretta and Yolanda."

I recognized Yolanda as the little girl with the red ball.

"Nice dress," she said. Coretta waved shyly, but stared at my dress, too.

Motioning to me, Samuel said, "This is my friend from school. Her name is Cassandra." Turning to me he added, "So, um, do you want to sit in the living room with me?"

I nodded and followed him into another really small room filled with a boxy tan sofa and two matching chairs pressed up against brown paneled walls. A braided oval rug lay in the middle of the off-white linoleum floor. I took a seat on the chair closest to me.

"Would you like some tea?" Samuel offered. I nodded. I was

thirsty. And hungry, but I didn't want to be rude and say so. Samuel turned out to be a great host, bringing me tea and cookies. I devoured the cookies in as ladylike a manner as possible. I was wearing this great dress and prim sandals, after all.

"That was brave of you what you did down there. Stupid but brave," Samuel said.

"Thanks?"

"Those are bad dudes. Bad luck to run into them."

Samuel sipped his tea, breathing deeply. We both were coming down from the adrenaline rush of our close encounter. I didn't want to think of the terrible things that could have happened. I hardly even had time to worry about Nate. I would be missing from the Watson Farm and he would think that I'd gone home without him.

Samuel leaned forward and spoke softly, "You're in trouble at home and at school and were planning on running away. I convinced you to come home with me so that my mother could help you and talk you out of it."

Ah, the story. "You think they'll believe that?"

"I don't know. But it will buy us some time."

"So, you live here with your mother and two little sisters?"

"And an older sister, Rosa." His face tensed when he mentioned her. "You'll meet her later. And my brother Jonah, he's fifteen."

"You really do have a brother Jonah?" He chuckled.

"Yeah, not there, though."

I felt travel exhaustion coming on, and suspected Samuel did, too. We needed to keep talking. It wouldn't do for me to fall asleep here, at least not until his mother was home. "What's going on around here? I know this is 1961, the first Civil Rights Act was introduced in 1957, but this is a northern state. Why the obvious segregation?"

Samuel leaned back and examined me. Uh, oh. I'd said too

much. "The first Civil Rights Act? What year are you from?" I glanced nervously toward the kitchen. "Don't worry. They're playing outside." Right. I'd heard the squeaky door.

"I come from, well, the future." That sounded so Sci- Fi! He believed me though.

"When?" He leaned forward again, deep interest in his eyes.

"I don't think I should say." I had to be careful. Samuel didn't have the advantage of having watched the Back to the Future trilogy to learn the hazards of knowing the future before you should.

"Give me a ball park. The nineteen eighties?"

"No." Thank God. I saw a picture of my mom with big puffy eighties hair. On second thought, I probably would've fit right in.

"Later?" I nodded my head. He gasped. "The year 2000?"

"A little more than that."

"Wow." He let out a low whistle. "Are there flying cars?"

"No. We still have to drive on the ground. Samuel, I'm not going to tell you about the future. Knowing things before you should would just hurt you."

He leaned back again. "I suppose you're right. But you can't blame me for being curious."

"Back to my question," I prodded.

"Oh, yes, well even though we don't have 'whites only' or 'colored only' signs here like they do in the south, there is still a lot tension between blacks and whites. We have black neighborhoods, black churches and even though our schools aren't officially segregated, the reality is much different."

I guess I knew this.

"Does it get better, Casey?" he whispered. I think he was afraid of the answer.

I hesitated. "In some ways, yes," I said thinking of the first African American president. And in some ways no, because we still had a lot of racial inequality in the world, but I didn't want to get into that. He accepted my silence on the subject.

The door squeaked and slammed.

"Rosa's home," he said. "And the plot thickens."

What could he mean by that?

"A little help here!" Rosa called. Alarm flashed over Samuel's face when he sprinted to her.

"Groceries?" I heard him say.

"Oh, sorry, Sam. I didn't mean that."

She spotted me peeking into the kitchen. Rosa was older than Samuel and almost the same height. Her hair was wrapped up under a colorful scarf. She had a pretty face, reminded me a bit of Alicia Keys, and a full beach ball-like stomach. That explained Samuel's initial concern. His sister Rosa was very due to have a baby.

"Who's she?" Rosa said, her eyes questioning and worried.

"She's a friend."

She turned her back and lowered her voice, but the apartment was so small I could still hear her. "Mama's gonna kill you, Sam."

"You're still alive."

Rosa opened up a cupboard and started emptying the contents of a brown paper bag. "I don't think her heart could take it again."

"It's not like that. She's really just a friend."

"Well, what are you waiting for? Introduce me."

I took that as my cue to enter the kitchen. Rosa's eyes scanned my face and then my dress.

"Uh, Rosa, this is my friend from school, Cassandra."

"Uh-huh." Rosa muttered. She didn't believe that lie for a minute.

"Cassandra, this is my older sister Rosa." I extended my hand, which surprised her, but she took it.

"Pleased to meet you," I said.

"Nice dress. I have one just like it."

My face flushed red. "Uh, well, we must like to shop in the same places."

She raised her eyebrows. "So, you're a friend from school."

I just nodded and realized I didn't even know the name of Samuel's school; I really hoped she didn't ask too many questions. I thought the best tactic was to turn the questioning back.

"So, you're pregnant. When's the baby due?"

You'd think I dropped a bomb in the room the way both Samuel and Rosa inhaled sharply. I realized I had just committed a cultural faux pas. I remembered now, having watched I Love Lucy reruns, that it wasn't polite or proper to say pregnant. You said expecting.

Rosa graciously recovered. "Any day. In fact I'm overdue."

"That's exciting." Rosa emptied the last bag. "I suppose. Obviously, you're a long way from home."

In more ways than one. Again, I just shrugged. Then she saw my eyes, the similar rings that Samuel had. Her head spun back to Samuel.

"Are you doing drugs, man?"

"No! Why would you say such a thing?"

"No offense, but you both look, uh, tired."

"Maybe we both are tired."

"Okay, okay. I'm just saying, if you're doing drugs...."

Rosa bent over with difficulty to get a pot out of a lower cupboard.

"We're not doing drugs, so just drop it." Samuel went to help her with the pot. "And Cassandra is staying for dinner."

"What about Mama?"

"I'll deal with her."

"It's your funeral."

When Rosa had her back turned, I motioned to Samuel with

my finger to follow me back to the living room. I spoke as low as humanly possible.

"I don't think this is a good idea."

"Do you have a better one?"

"What is your mother going to do? I don't want you to get into trouble."

"Don't worry. Rosa has made enough trouble for us all. She makes the rest of us look like saints."

"Because of the..." I pointed to my stomach. He nodded.

"Not married?"

He shook his head. "No." Right. In this era it was a great disgrace to be an unwed mother.

"No father?"

"Oh, there's a father all right. But he's white."

"I guess that's a bad thing?"

"No kidding."

"Why didn't they get married?"

"Man, Cassandra, things must be different where you come from. It's illegal for white and black to marry. That's why my mama's going to have a fit when she sees you. She'll think that...."

"Oh." That we were a couple. "But we're not."

"She'll believe us eventually."

The door creaked open and the chatter of two little girls entered along with the admonishing voice of a woman who must be "Mama." Rosa had something cooking that smelled really good, and she commanded everyone to wash up for supper. I dreaded the inquisition that was to come. Mama didn't see me at first. She went straight to Samuel and looked into his eyes. The circles had diminished, but were still evident.

"Baby, you should see a doctor. That's not normal."

"I'm fine, Mama."

Then she saw me.

Mama was a big woman, with full breasts and large eyes that squinted into snakelike slits as she examined my presence.

"Samuel?" she said, not taking her eyes off me. I was scared of Mama.

"Mama, this is Cassandra. She's a friend from school."

She turned back to Samuel. "Are you crazy? Don't we have enough trouble with Rosa, and now, you bring home a white girl?"

"She's in trouble, she needs our help."

"Our help? Our help? Her white folks are going to call their white cops and her white daddy's lawyer is going to have us arrested for kidnapping! Are you out of your mind?"

Just then the door squealed again. Samuel's younger brother walked in. "What's going on?"

Rosa answered, "Hey, Jonah. Samuel brought home a white girl."

Jonah lowered his head. "Not again."

"It's not like that!" I blurted. They all swiveled to look at me. My underarms started sweating. "I'm sorry. I don't want to cause any trouble. Really, we're just friends. I already have a boyfriend."

Well, in my dreams, I did. Their combined looks of doubt made me add, "He lives in another town." I had a stroke of inspiration. "That's why I'm in trouble."

Samuel's family inhaled in unison. This was a problem they understood. As much as I'd like to leave Samuel and his family in peace, I needed him to get me back to Nate.

Poor Nate! He must be freaking. And what if someone tried to make him join the army? I had to get back. Like it or not, I was Samuel's shadow. After dinner, which lasted all of five minutes— you'd think the Jones kids only got to eat every second day—I asked Samuel about Jerome.

"We just left them waiting."

"Oh, they're probably all drunk in their beds by now. Don't worry about them."

Mama called a family meeting. No one was to mention my presence in the home to anyone, in the complex or at school. Even Yolanda and Coretta seemed to understand the importance of Mama's command. The black/white divide started young.

Rosa and her sisters slept together in one room, the little girls in wooden bunk beds and Rosa on a single bed less than two feet on the other side of the room. To accommodate me, Coretta climbed in with Yolanda on the top bunk. Samuel and Jonah shared the only other bedroom across the hall and to my surprise, Mama pulled out bedding from the closet and slept on the living room couch. There weren't enough bedrooms to go around.

I curled up under the covers, wearing nightclothes Rosa had lent me. A streetlight shone in through the window and I could see Rosa's face clearly. The breathing of the girls above me had already settled into a heavy rhythm; through the wall the muffled sounds of a married couple fighting.

"Don't mind them," Rosa whispered.

"They fight every night. I just block it out of my mind."

I kept my voice low. "It's okay. I'm used to rolling with the punches."

Her forehead wrinkled. "Someone beating you, girl?"

"Oh, no, it's a figure of speech. It means my circumstances change a lot. I'm used to adapting."

"You said you got boyfriend troubles?"

"Sorta." Here was my chance. "Do you?"

She laughed softly; edged with bitterness. "You definitely could say that."

"What happened, if you don't mind me asking?" After talking to Samuel, I had a clue.

"Oh, the usual sad story. He said he loved me. I believed him. When it came to proving the words, he was gone like a mad dog."

"Samuel said he was white."

"As the driven snow. I sure was sweet on him, though."

I was curious. "How'd you meet?"

"My mama and me, we work at the local motel as chamber-maids. Patrick, well he was going through a rebellious spot. Only child he is, and smothered half to death by his parents. Patrick thought he could make it on his own, out from under the shadow of his rich daddy. He owns the fish cannery down by the docks.

"So, Patrick, he thought he would try selling them encyclope-dias, door to door. He lived at the motel. Well, we'd pass each other in the hallways, and then he'd start saying hi and looking at me like he was interested, y'know? Then one day he asked if I wanted to go for lunch. The rest is history, as they say."

Rosa glanced over to see if I was still awake and listening. I think she enjoyed telling her story to someone she didn't plan on seeing again. "When I found out I was, well, with child, Patrick went crazy. He said he'd find a way for me to get rid of it."

"Is that possible?"

"It's illegal, of course," Rosa continued, "But it's possible if you have the right connections. Which I don't. I've heard stories of girls who died in the hands of would-be doctors in some back alley warehouse."

Scary.

"I admit I thought about it. How nice it would be just to 'undo' this. Go on with life like I didn't fall in love, didn't make any mistakes at all. Not to have to trouble my family with the shame and gossip and extra expense we can hardly afford." She paused, pensive.

"But..." I prodded.

"My daddy drove a taxi."

I was confused by her sudden change of topic. She contin-ued, "One night a white guy decided he didn't have to pay a black man what he'd earned. Stabbed him with a knife."

"Rosa! That's terrible. Did he...?"

"Yes. My daddy's dead. Yolanda was only two years old. Mama, me and the boys we had to get jobs to make up for Daddy's paycheck. We've been working ever since."

"Where does Samuel work?"

"Oh, he's the janitor of this complex." He's the janitor. I smiled to myself.

"So, Patrick, well, he said he was sorry, that he really did love me, but what could he do? He couldn't marry me, could he? And his father would disinherit him if he found out about us. Ending, uh, this," she pointed to her belly, "was the only way out.

"Well, I say to him, the only reason my daddy was killed was because of the color of his skin. I wouldn't kill this baby just because his mama's and daddy's skin color don't match."

She sighed heavily. "I told him he was a coward and to get out of my life."

I thought of Tyson and Kelly. No one would bother them because their skin wasn't the same color. I was certain that those two would be an official item in no time at all. Rosa rubbed her big tummy.

"Are you keeping the baby, Rosa?" I heard a sniff. When I looked at her, a tear coursed down her cheek.

"I want to, Cassandra. I really wish I could, but I don't see how. I'd have to stay home to take care of the child, and we need all the money we can earn to survive. If we don't make the rent, there's another family on the wait list who will grab this apartment in a second. Plus, it ain't no good raising a baby without a father. Just ask my mama."

NINETEEN

ROSA WHIPPED UP SCRAMBLED eggs and toast to feed all of us at breakfast. I felt bad that I was eating their food, knowing how hard they all had to work for it. Mama had already left for her job. Fortunately, it was Sunday, so Samuel didn't have to go to school. I don't know how I would've managed to shadow him there.

"I have to work today, Cassandra."

"I'll help." He nodded, understanding I needed to stay close. Then I remembered the thugs I'd outwitted the night before. Actually, despite Samuel's reassurances, I was surprised they hadn't come to this apartment. Then I thought of Mama. Maybe it wasn't so surprising. I'd bet this whole complex was afraid of her. Still, she wasn't here now.

"Um, Samuel, what about those boys from yesterday?"

"Jerome and his idiots? Don't worry about them. They don't get out of bed until dinner time."

We started in the building next to the one the Joneses lived in. Samuel had to sweep and mop all the common areas, including the main entrance where the post boxes were. There wasn't any carpeting, just light-colored pattern linoleum with a gray path worn from the door to the mailboxes and up the stairs. The soapy disinfectant Samuel used to scrub the floors helped to erase the unpleasant stale smell.

I stuck as close as humanly possible, only bumping into him twice so far.

"How often between trips, usually?" I said, while wiping the railing with a wet cloth.

"Sometimes two days, sometimes two weeks, sometimes two months, sometimes longer. I never know when it's going to happen."

The anxiety I felt for Nate tightened my chest steadily. I needed to get back ASAP.

"Do you find anything in particular that triggers it? I mean, with me it seems to be stress. It can be good stress or bad, but when my heart gets going over something, boom, I'm a goner."

Samuel brushed dirt from the steps into a dustpan and tossed it into the garbage can. "I suppose. Seems like life is always about some kind of stress. I don't like going back. It's a worse time for blacks in the last century than it is in this one."

He paused to pick up a cigarette butt off the floor. "I'm afraid I'm going to die there. Then what would happen to my family?" He was afraid because of how his absence would hurt his family, not because he feared dying. I couldn't help but admire him. I'm sure he had a lot of admirers, probably a dozen alone living in this complex.

"You got a girlfriend, Samuel?"

He huffed. "I don't have room in my life for a girlfriend. Even if I did, how could I, you know, be close to someone without taking her...without endangering her life?"

I nodded. I felt the same way about Nate. Thinking of him made my stomach spin webs of worry. What was he doing now? Was he afraid I'd left him in the past forever?

We were on the second floor when Yolanda burst into the lobby, calling out for Samuel. "Sam! Sam!"

"Up here!" he shouted down.

"Sam, come quick. It's Rosa!"

We both dropped everything and ran down the stairs. Yolanda slipped by a tall dark shadow just before he blocked the doorway.

"Get out of the way, Jerome!" Samuel shouted.

Jerome grabbed my arm. "You didn't keep your promise." His breath was rancid.

"Let her go!" Samuel rushed at Jerome, even though Jerome was larger. He wrapped his arm around Samuel's neck, letting go of me to do so. I jumped on his back like a monkey. Jerome loosened up on Samuel just enough that he was able to pull away. Jerome shook me off his back, pulling me to his chest, and wrapped both arms around me tight.

"You can go, Sammy boy, but it's my turn with your white whore."

What did he just call me? I had Rosa's spiky shoes on, and even with my toes hanging over the front edge, I could slam the pointy heel down on the top of Jerome's canvas sneaker. Which I did. Hard. Jerome let out a grizzly bellow and fell back against the mailboxes. Samuel grabbed my hand and pulled. "Come on!"

We were panting when we got to the Joneses apartment. And we weren't the only ones. Rosa lay on her back on the rug in the living room. Her face was purple and glistened with sweat.

"Sam, the baby's coming."

"Did someone call the ambulance?" I said.

"We can't afford a hospital, Cassandra," Samuel answered. "Has someone gone for Mama?"

Rosa's panting kept her from answering.

"Coretta's gone for her," Yolanda said, standing in the corner trembling.

I quickly put my arms around her and gave her a squeeze. "Your mama will be here soon."

I could see panic rise in Samuel's face.

"It's okay, Samuel," I added bravely. "I've helped to deliver a baby before."

I took charge, praying that Mama would burst through the squeaky door any moment. "Yolanda, sweetie, put the kettle on the stove and then bring me clean towels."

Rosa cried out in pain. Samuel grabbed my arm, tighter than he meant to. I really didn't want to deliver another baby. I'd almost fainted with the last one.

"I think it's coming!" she shouted.

Then the miracle I prayed for happened. Actually, two miracles. First, the door sprung open and Mama bounded in. Then Samuel pulled me into the kitchen and I felt him quiver as we disappeared into the light.

When the dizziness stopped, I let go of Samuel. I had my "nightgown" dress back on, though he still wore his own clothes from the sixties. We were in the middle of a grove of trees, the way nature was before the apartment complex Samuel lived in was built.

"Wow," I said. "What a rush."

"It was a wild ride," he said softly.

"I'm sorry, Samuel. I know that was a bad time to leave."

"It's okay. I'd probably just be in the way anyway. Besides, I'm not going to miss a thing."

I smiled. He was right, of course. When he returned the only thing missing would be me. "I'll walk you back," Samuel said. I was happy to comply, since he seemed to know the way. Before I knew it, we stood by the water pump right where we'd left.

"I gotta go now," Samuel said.

"You're not staying? Cobbs is gone."

"I know, but I've met other good people who'll look out for me. I like to spread myself around."

He glanced shyly at his feet. "It was good getting to know you, Cassandra."

"Bye, Samuel." I couldn't let him go without giving him a hug. I swallowed hard as I watched him disappear into the forest. I might never see Samuel again.

TWENTY

I WAS BACK. And I needed to find Nate.

I sprinted to the cabin and flung open the door calling his name. Beds unmade, gray ashes in the fireplace, but no Nate. I checked behind the cabin and knocked on the outhouse. No sign. I headed to the barn, lifting my skirt as I trekked down the path, my anticipation growing with each step. That must be where he was.

The barn door was stuck open part way, far enough for me to squeeze through. A waft of horse manure and stale hay tickled my senses. Stopping to pet a chestnut colored mare, I whispered in her ear, "Have you seen Nate anywhere, huh, honey?" I inhaled deeply of her sweaty horsiness.

"Hello." Nate leaned against the wall behind me, his arms crossed. I was giddy to see him and felt like throwing myself into his arms. Which would've been hard to do, what with his arms crossed like that.

"Nate, are you okay?"

"I am now that I know I haven't been abandoned. I actually

thought I'd be waiting a lot longer for you to come back. I have to say, it's not a good feeling. Being stuck here."

"I'm sorry, Nate." My mood dropped from giddy to depressed in ten seconds flat. Nate hadn't worried about me at all. He'd only cared about what would happen to him—which was totally understandable, given the circumstances. But, still.

"Are my parents worried? How did you explain my absence?"

Though the distance between us was only a few feet, it suddenly felt like a huge chasm. I couldn't guess how Nate would take this new piece of news, that there are others like me in this universe and that there was a chance I could potentially travel in new loops. That info might just push him over the edge. Honestly, I was just waiting for some breaker switch to go off and for him to bolt as far from me as possible.

"Casey?"

"Well, actually, I didn't go back, uh, there."

Nate shifted his weight. "What do you mean?"

"You remember Samuel?"

"Yeah," he said tentatively.

"Well, I ran into him again, at the well."

Nate stubbornly kept his face blank, "And?"

"So, I fell or maybe I fainted, and then he caught my arm."

Nate exhaled heavily. "Casey, you're killing me. Just spit it out."

"He's like me," I whispered. "He's a traveler."

I didn't know what he expected, but by the heavy wrinkles in his forehead and the contorted expression on his no longer blank face, it wasn't that.

"Y-you traveled with him?"

I nodded.

"Where to?" I knew he meant when to, but that is just too weird to say.

"Nineteen sixty-one."

He stopped. "Nineteen sixty-one!"

I nodded weakly. Nate paced in a small circle, kicking up dust and straw bits. He ran his hand through his hair, his eyes wide and looking kind of wild. I took a deep breath and continued.

"Samuel is a traveler, like me. His present is 1961, but he loops to the same year I do."

Nate stopped and looked at me. "Okay, so what happened there? Where did you sleep?"

Where did I sleep? Did he think I spent the night cuddling with Samuel? I suppose it could've been a possibility if we were stranded somewhere, and it was cold, but....

"I slept with his sisters. He has three."

He breathed out, and looked away. His fists were clenching and, though I really wanted to know what he was thinking, I had to answer his questions first.

"Samuel gave me one of his sister's dresses. Rosa. She was pregnant and didn't fit her regular clothes anyway."

The horse whinnied in my ear, startling me. I caught my breath and kept going. "They live in an apartment complex for blacks."

"All blacks?" Nate whispered, raising his eyebrows. I nodded.

"How'd that work for you?"

"I kept a low profile. You know I'm good at that." I decided to leave out the bit about Jerome and his groupies. "Anyway, the Joneses are cool with white people. In fact Rosa had a white boyfriend."

"Had?"

"Yeah, well, that's how she got pregnant. Not a great scene, really. Rosa told me she was giving up the baby for adoption."

Nate shook his head. "Look, Casey. I need some air. I'm going to go for a walk, okay?"

"Sure," I nodded, feeling sick inside. I watched him leave,

certain that it was over between us. Whatever "it" was. I turned back to the mare, needing comfort.

A board in the loft creaked with the weight of a man. I jumped back, squealing with fright. Someone descended. My heart froze.

Robert Willingsworth scooted down the makeshift ladder.

"What are you doing here?" I said, once I found my voice.

"The better question, my darling, is what are you doing?"

He smirked. "I saw you through a crack in the loft, hugging that colored boy."

"If you're here for Cobbs," I said, "then you'll be disappointed. As you can imagine, the Watsons fired him."

"Yes, I figured that." He took a step toward me. I involuntarily took a step back.

"He's probably drunk in the tavern, the uncivilized lout. But, it's true, I was hoping to find him, he has been helpful in the past." He chuckled, while petting the mare. I realized belatedly, she must have been his.

"That was quite the story you told that idiot brother of yours. Do you think he actually believed that?"

I gulped. How much had he heard? Robert's eyes scanned my face and my body, filling with something ugly.

"Actually, it's quite serendipitous, to find you here. Alone." He took another step forward, stroking his mustache in consideration. "You know, you owe me."

"I owe you?" I said, taking another awkward step back. "For what?"

"For reneging on a promise. Oh yes, and for publicly humiliating me. Do you know what kind of scorn I had to endure when word got around that you had, in the end, refused me?"

I totally didn't give one hoot about his public scorning. Robert took another step toward me, I took another step back. Okay, now I was afraid. He wasn't strong like Cobbs in an old ox kind of way but he wasn't a wimp either. There was no way I could take him, especially in this stupid dress. Worse yet, he had backed me into a corner.

"I'm going to scream," I whispered. He moved in closer. I took another tentative step back, my hand grabbing at air behind me hoping to find a shovel or pick. Anything I could use to protect myself.

"Nate," I coughed. My throat closed up.

"Oh, he's left you," Robert said with a twisted, evil grin. "I watched him go from the window in the loft. My guess is your "brother" doesn't want to share you with your colored friend."

Robert's face pressed up to mine. I could smell his cologne and smoky breath and it made me gag. "But I don't mind."

"Back off, Robert!" I thrust my hands into his chest and pushed. He grabbed my arms with one hand and I found my voice, screaming for Nate. I squirmed and kicked—he put his other disgusting hand over my mouth.

"This is what I like about you, Cassandra. You're so spirited." He leaned in to kiss me, and I almost burst into tears. I didn't have a chance to think beyond that because suddenly Robert was off me.

Appearing like magic, Nate pulled Robert away and right-hooked him in the chin. Robert stumbled, but righted himself and charged, thrusting Nate against the side of the barn.

"Nate!" He pushed Robert off and sneaked in a left stab to the gut. Robert keeled over and fell. Nate ran to me, pulling me close.

"Casey, are you all right?"

I didn't have a chance to answer. Robert lunged from behind and they both fell to the ground, rolling back and forth. I spied a shovel. I grabbed it. Nate and Robert still wrestled in the hay. Now, I just had to make sure I hit the right head.

Normally, I'm pretty coordinated. Even though I hide it well,

I can shoot a basketball into the hoop. I can run in a straight line. I can hunt quail with a slingshot. But normally I'm not surging adrenaline while watching someone I care for a lot fight a thug to save my life. Normally, I'm not wearing a nightgown in a barn with obstacles such as a bucket of oats hidden in the hay.

From my peripheral I could see Nate. He was on top of Robert and winning. I saw this while tripping over the bucket, my skirt twisting between my legs. Even in this split second my mind assessed my surroundings. I'd fall in the hay, I'd be fine.

I was wrong.

TWENTY-ONE

PITCH BLACKNESS. A rhythmic pulsing. Tandem shots of pain, slight at first like striking matches, growing steadily into fireworks. I heard Nate's voice from a faraway place. Cas-ey, Casey! My lips had dried out, so my desire to screech "ouch" resembled something more like an injured wild animal.

"Casey?"

"Oh, my head," I moaned. The throbbing intensified, and I fought the urge to retreat back into the darkness. My memory kicked in; the last image was of Nate fighting.

"Nate?"

"Yes, I'm here."

"Are you okay?" I asked.

"You're asking me if I'm okay? You're the one who knocked herself out."

I tried to sit up, but my head revolted with a throbbing blast of pain. Plus, my arm really hurt. For the first time I saw the blood. It was on my skirt and in the hay.

"Where's it coming from?" I muttered.

Nate was busy ripping off his shirt. Even in my dazed condition, I could tell he had a very nice thing going on with his chest. Still, I was a little fuzzy as to why Nate was ripping his shirt to shreds while I lay bleeding to death. He solved the puzzle by wrapping my left forearm tightly with a piece of his shirt.

"Looks like you sliced it on the shovel when you fell." His face darkened with concern. "You'll need stitches. When was the last time you had a tetanus shot?"

I couldn't remember. Then Nate took a strip and gently wrapped it around my head. Blood was oozing from there, too.

"Quite the goose egg you got there, Casey."

"Thanks. I'm going for a new look."

He smiled. "Any look looks good on you, but I should get you to the house. You need a doctor."

The pain that surged through my body when he lifted me into his arms confirmed that assessment, though I had to say, I didn't mind the feeling of being carried by Nate. I had a mental image of him pounding the tar out of Robert Willingsworth.

A thin jolt of fear stabbed me. "Where's Robert?"

"I knocked his lights out then tied him to a hitching post. We'll deal with him later."

Nate managed to open the kitchen door of the Watson house with his fingers and carry me into the house without knocking my head on the doorframe. Working on the farm was making Nate strong! In the kitchen we were greeted by a handful of kids. Nate sat me in a chair.

"Can you get Sara or your mother?" Nate said.

Josephine, who was about thirteen, answered, "They're not here. They took a carriage to take food to a neighbor. They left me in charge of the kids, said they'd only be gone a couple hours."

"Okay, Josephine," said Nate "Where's the ice?"

"Uh, there's no ice here, Nate." I mumbled. "Eighteen hundreds remember?"

"We have to get your arm stitched up."

"Who's going to do that?"

"Sara?"

"Josephine just said they would be a while. Will I live until they get back?"

"This sucks, Casey. I'm afraid it might get infected. That would be bad."

Very bad. "I guess you have to do it then."

"Me? I'm no doctor."

"And I don't think I can let you do it without freezing it. I don't like pain, and it already hurts like crazy."

Nate paced the kitchen, and then filled a pot with water. He started the fire in the stove. I think he scared the kids, because they took off.

"Are you making tea?"

"Very funny."

"I'm not joking."

"I'm boiling water so I can disinfect a needle."

"Do you have a sewing kit?"

"I don't, but someone around here must. It's serious, Casey, you need stitches."

He was so intense and caring. It made me smile. Then laugh. Then cry. It hurt my head when I laughed. Pain and trauma induced giddiness overcame me.

"Casey!"

"I'm sorry, Nate. Come here." I sounded like a drunkard. "Please."

Maybe I had a concussion. He was down on his knees in front of me in an instant. I wrapped my good arm around his neck. It's not only that I wanted to hug him, though of course I did. It was that I felt a tunnel of bright light coming on.

We were back at the school library, back in our normal clothes. Nate holding me in his arms, and me in need of a doctor, pronto. All around us were gasps from other students. I could hear them whisper, "What happened to her?"

Nate didn't pay them any attention. He carried me through the library, past all the turning heads, down the hall and to the nurse's lounge. So embarrassing. We hadn't had a chance to come up with the story. It looked like I'd gotten beat up, but in the library?

"I fell," I said, leaving it at that. The nurse gave me a cold press to put on my head, which I held in place with my good arm. She shook her head upon seeing my other arm.

"I'm afraid you're going to need a doctor for that." She poured antiseptic on it and wrapped it in gauze. "Is there someone you can call to take you to the hospital?"

"I'll call my mom." The nurse handed me a phone and I dialed. "Mom?" I said, when she answered. "Now don't freak out, but I need a ride to the hospital."

"What happened?" she said, her voice noticeably higher. "I fell. It's not that big of a deal, but I think I need a couple stitches."

"I'll come right away, but I'm with a client about an hour and a half away. Is that okay?"

"I'll take you," Nate said. Obviously, he could hear her. She was talking really loudly.

"Mom, it's okay. I have a friend who can take me."

"Yes, you should get there as soon as possible. I'll meet you there."

Nate helped me to his car and buckled me in, as it was kind of hard for me to do it with one hand. I checked out my reflection in the vanity mirror on the back of the sun visor. My face was vampire pale, my eyes bloodshot from the hay and my hair sprung out like a wool mop. I was a horror.

We arrived at the hospital parking lot. Nate cut the engine. "You fell off the outdoor bleachers at school."

Another story. Sounded good to me. Nate got out then

opened my door and helped me. We checked in. I had my Social Security Card in my backpack, which I had sent Nate back to the library to retrieve, and waited in the lobby until a doctor could see me. The nurse called my name. Nate came with me like he was my boyfriend or something. He was acting very strange, possessive, yet trying really hard to stay distant.

I yipped when the first needle went in my arm, but once the area was frozen, I was fine. Just an annoying tugging at my skin as the doctor stitched my wound. Mom stormed in just as we were checking out.

"Casey! Oh my goodness. That looks like more than a couple of stitches to me."

Nate stepped back out of her way.

"Yeah, there are six stitches. I fell off the bleachers."

Then to derail her from further scrutiny. "Mom, this is Nate. He drove me here."

Mom shifted her attention to him. "Thank you, Nate. It was really kind of you to go out of your way."

"I was glad to," he said. "Well, I guess, Casey you're in good hands now?"

Mom jumped in, "Yes, let's get you home."

I hated leaving Nate with such an informal good-bye, especially after all we'd just gone through. His shoulders slumped as he walked back to his car. He'd had enough of me and my freaky, trippy life. York University probably looked really good to him right about now. A pain jagged my heart, sharper than anything my physical body had experienced. On the ride home, my hand went to my neck, my fingers searching but not finding anything.

"Oh no," I groaned.

"Honey, is something wrong. Do you need to go back to the hospital?"

"No, I'm fine, it's my necklace. The one Dad got me for my birthday. It's gone."

"Oh no," Mom said. "Did it fall off at the bleachers?"

More likely it broke off when I fell in the hay. Could this day get any worse? Mom helped me out of the car. Once inside, I made my way into the kitchen and sat down. Mom poured me some juice.

"So that Nate? Who is he?"

There was another question implied. Was that Nate someone special?

"He's just a guy from my school." How's that for a colossal understatement! "He was there when I fell, so he drove me to the doctor."

She sat down across from me. "You look really tired. You should go upstairs and rest. Are you hungry? I'll bring you a sandwich."

"Okay, thanks." I plopped backside on my bed, stared at the white speckled ceiling and heaved a heavy sigh. I thought about the Jones family, how cool it had been to meet them, and that quite possibly, some of them might still be alive, though it would be wrong for me to seek them out. Even if they remembered me, I wouldn't have changed in over fifty years. I wondered how Rosa did with the delivery, if the baby was okay. Then I thought about Robert and how terrified I had been. I let myself dwell on what could have happened if Nate hadn't been there to save me and shuddered.

The thing was, he technically shouldn't have been there with me. And even though Nate was the victor with Robert Willingsworth, another time he could be the one to get hurt. Even killed. I couldn't risk that. He might be letting me go, but I had to let him go, too.

TWENTY-TWO

"THEY SAY RELATIONSHIPS forged in a crisis never work." Lucinda was counseling me between Algebra and Bio. "For example, remember the movie we watched on HBO called Speed?"

I grunted, "Kind of."

"Well, the cute girl and the hot guy have to keep a bus over a certain speed limit or a bomb that is planted underneath will go off. They bond during this near death, hours long crisis, and by the end of the movie they are 'together'."

"Okay, yeah, now I remember."

We moved down the crowded hallway. It was getting warmer and most of the kids had switched to short sleeve shirts. I always wore long sleeves at school. Too much bumping and shoving going on.

Lucinda kept talking. "So, then comes Speed Two. Same idea except with a cruise ship. The cute girl is back but no hot guy. The reason? The cute girl says relationships forged in a crisis never work or something to that effect."

"Luce, your point?"

"It's like that for you and Nate. You bonded during an unusual circumstance. A type of crisis."

"Are you trying to encourage me, or should I go slit my wrists?"

"Casey! I'm saying, face up to facts and move on." Is this what they called tough love? I hated her right now. But she was right.

"Thanks for the pep talk. I'm going to move on. Starting right now." Still, I couldn't help looking for him. He hadn't shown up at my locker that morning, not for a casual hi, not even to inquire about my health. As I waited for my Bio class to start, I checked my schedule for English and frowned. Last class.

Lucinda sat down beside me and pushed her stool a little too close to mine, accidentally brushing against my bad arm.

"Ouch," I squeaked. The bandaged peeked out from underneath my sleeve.

"What happened to you?" she said.

"I fell."

Her eyes went all squinty. "I heard that Nate had to carry a girl to the nurse's office from the library yesterday. Was that you?"

I nodded. "Yes."

Lucinda's brow furrowed, "So, you fell in the library?"

Ashley dropped her books on the desk on the other side of mine. "I heard about that, too. That was you?"

Oh, brother. Good thing my mop of curly hair covered the massive bump there. "I tripped and caught my arm on a jagged edge of a table. It's no big deal."

Ashley's mouth formed a goofy smile. "How'd it feel to be carried by Nate Mackenzie?"

"It was awesome, except for the slice in my arm and the throbbing, bleeding part."

Lucinda hissed into my ear, "You traveled with him again, didn't you?"

Mr. Pybus called class to order. I was glad to be out from under Lucinda's magnifying glass. She pulled her stool farther away from me. I couldn't believe she was mad over this.

Nate wasn't at the jock table at lunch. That's when I knew for sure (probably), that he was avoiding me. It was hard for me to eat; not much room for food when my stomach had a big nervous rock in it. The new girl, Kelly, sat with Tyson. She giggled and he grabbed her porcelain hand, weaving his dark fingers through hers. I knew they were going to get together. It made me think of Rosa and the heartache she'd suffered just because she was black and Patrick was white.

Lucinda looked like she wasn't even going to sit with me. I grabbed her arm and forced her into a chair. "Why are you freaking on me?"

"I'm not freaking." She flicked her hair.

"Yes. You. Are. Look, Lucinda, I really need your friendship right now. I can't deal with this PMS thing you got going on with Nate."

Lucinda's jaw tightened. She wouldn't look me in the eye. "Luce? Come on?" I prodded. Her eyes grew glassy, and I thought she might start crying right in the cafeteria. She forced a smile.

"I just feel stupidly jealous that you are having this life with Nate, an adventure, and that I'm not a part of it. I feel left out, like you don't tell me anything anymore."

"Lucinda, I'm sorry," I said. "I know I've been preoccupied lately. I didn't mean to shut you out, or keep secrets. I wish you were part of my crazy other world."

"Really?"

"Duh, yeah." I reached and squeezed her hand. Skin to skin.

We both sucked in a breath. Nothing happened. I smiled and let go. "See, it's just not meant to be."

The corners of Lucinda's lips curled. "Wow. When you did that, I thought you were crazy, Case. Thanks for trying, but in all honesty, I'm glad nothing happened. I want to and I don't want to, you know? It's dumb."

"It's an unusual situation, and it's not dumb," I said. "So, we're good again?"

Lucinda lifted her sandwich to her mouth. "We're good."

My Nate radar never rested, and I had my first sighting after fourth period. He was walking away from me, and I could see that he was looking down talking to someone shorter than him, but his body blocked my view and I couldn't see who until he turned the corner.

It was Jessica. She giggled and pushed her strawberry blond hair behind her ear, then patted his arm. I felt sick. He'd gone back to her. Safe, predictable, fun-loving, pretty (stupid), Jessica. My world cracked open and I felt myself falling in.

I thought for sure that seeing them together would stress me to the point of tripping, but it didn't. Geez, I was the most unpredictable person alive, even to myself.

But, next came English. How was I to survive that? I entered through the back door of the classroom. Nate was already in his seat, his back to me, and didn't see me come in. Mr. Turner called the class to order and then I held my breath and waited. Would Nate turn to see if I was there? Seconds ticked by. Then, he did it. He turned slowly, and raised his chin in acknowledgment before turning his attention back to Mr. Turner.

Mr. Turner handed out worksheets on William Shakespeare-The Man, and the whole class was devoted to that. I couldn't concentrate. I could barely breathe. Nate had looked at me. It meant he didn't hate me entirely.

Mercifully, the bell rang. I fully expected Nate to high tail it out of class before he could run into me. He surprised me by coming to my desk.

"We should talk about it," he said as I gathered up my books.

"Okay. Now?"

"Can't. Baseball practice. After that?"

"Sure, what time?"

"Seven o'clock. I'll come to your house."

I nodded, forcing down the dread. I really wished we could get this over with. Seven o'clock was a long way away.

After school I packed up my homework, swung my backpack over my shoulder and walked with Lucinda past the baseball diamond.

"I think I like basketball season best," Lucinda said. "You don't have to worry about the weather, or squint through the sun to see a cute guy's face. Everything is nice and close."

"Sports are all consuming for some people."

"Meaning Nate?" Lucinda pushed a pair of sunglasses onto her face. I followed suit—the spring glare was blinding. "How was English today?"

"He wants to talk after baseball."

"That's good." She saw my face. "Isn't it?"

"I don't know. Something happened..."

"I knew it. You are secretly dating."

"Lucinda, honestly, if Nate was more than a friend to me, I wouldn't be hiding it from you. I wouldn't hide it from anyone. I'd shout it from the mountain tops, so stop acting like I'm dating on the sly."

"Hey, I'm just joking."

I ignored her. Lucinda swung her arm around my shoulders giving me a quick squeeze. "I'm sorry. I don't mean to be insensitive. You know I'm rooting for you, right? I just want whatever makes you happy."

At that moment, Nate caught the ball, and then looked up

from across the field spotting me. He paused before throwing the ball back to the pitcher.

"I'm sorry, too, Luce. I know I've been a nut case lately."

Her cell phone rang, and Lucinda dug through her purse looking for it.

I pointed to my watch and mouthed, "Later."

She nodded, while answering her phone and mouthed back "Call me," meaning after the talk.

On the bus I daydreamed about the coming meeting, imagining all the ways Nate could back out of our friendship. It was like we were breaking up, even though we'd never actually gone out. It would be the "non break-up" break-up.

What speech would he choose? The "it's not you, it's me," speech, or a revised version of the library talk. "I thought I was stronger, Casey, but I can't do this anymore. Besides, I have my future to look out for and let's face it, I'm leaving for Toronto soon."

When the bus stopped at my stop, I was thoroughly depressed. And thirsty. The sun beat down on my head, and my throat was parched. It could've been a result of the heat, or it could've been the effort I was putting into holding back tears. Without thinking I walked into the convenience store, welcoming the blast of air-conditioning, and headed straight for the refrigerated drinks. My arm reached out to grab a dark soda, nearly missing contact with another whiter arm.

"Oh, excuse me," I said.

The girl had long blond hair pulled into a ponytail and bright-red glossy lipstick on her lips. She wore a colorful retro dress—it reminded me of the one I'd borrowed from Rosa— with a short jacket that didn't match and flat tie up shoes. She flashed me a wide smile, revealing straight, white teeth.

"No problem, you go ahead," she said.

"Thanks." I took a soda, handing it to the girl. "Is this the one you wanted?"

"Yes, that's great. It's so hot out today. I'm just dying of thirst." She accepted the can revealing a handmade beaded bracelet on her wrist. Alphabet beads spelled the name "Adeline."

I took a second soda for myself and watched as Adeline walked the aisles nonchalantly and then scanned the candy bar rack. She had ear buds in I hadn't noticed right away and she started singing, aloud, right there in the store. Crooner-type music, maybe Michael Bublé, and she had a pretty good voice, too. I had to admire her, the carefree way she dressed and her unrestrained public singing. Like she couldn't care less what anyone else thought of her.

A pang of envy gripped me. Why couldn't I be like her? Why couldn't I just be a normal girl? I got in line to pay and Adeline followed in behind me, soda can in hand. I guessed she'd decided against the candy bar. She flicked a strand of blond out of her eyes.

The cashier rung in my order and I plunked a five-dollar bill on the counter. I collected my change and turned slightly towards Adeline, behind me. Her eyes were different. The previous sparkle had disappeared and she seemed disoriented.

And she had dark rings. She opened her hand, peering at the change resting in her palm, before laying it out on the counter. Then she walked purposefully out the door, all the carefree attitude of a moment ago, gone.

"Hey! Wait a minute." I ran after her. "Adeline?" She spun on her heel.

"Do I know you?"

"Uh, no. I saw your bracelet." She checked her watch and peered down the street.

"Oh, well, I have to catch a bus." She walked on, and I

followed her. I tried to put myself in her shoes. I supposed I could come off as a bit of a wild-haired stalker.

I softened my voice, "I was just wondering, um, did you just go somewhere?" This was tricky.

"We're all going somewhere, aren't we?"

"I know, it's just, I noticed your eyes." She looked down, self-conscious. "I mean, it happens to me, too. I uh, go places. I get rings under my eyes."

I sounded like an idiot. I couldn't bring myself to say I'm a time traveler. She'd think I was on drugs for sure. Unless I was right and she was one, too.

She stopped and stared. "What do you mean, go places?"

"Well, sometimes, I feel this dizziness and a bright flash of light, and I trip...."

"You fall down?"

"No, by trip I mean I travel."

Her eyes widened. "You're a traveler?"

I nodded, keeping my expression friendly in a non-psycho way.

"Time?"

"Yes, I travel through time."

She turned and continued walking. Maybe I'd missed something. Did I read the signs wrong? We arrived at the bus stop and she slid onto an empty bench. I sat beside her, keeping enough space between us.

"So, when you *trip*, to when do you go?" she said.

"The eighteen hundreds."

Her left eyebrow shot up. "Really? Wow. And I thought I had it bad. How's that, anyway?"

I shrugged. "Okay, I guess."

"I hang in the nineteen fifties. But my dad and I are moving to California soon, and I'm worried."

"I get that," I said. "It's hard enough when you know what to expect. It's the reason I never go anywhere. I'm a non-traveler on this side of things."

Maybe Adeline had the answers I wanted. "Do you know why?" I said. "Why you, uh, we, travel? Is there some cosmic point, or something?"

Adeline considered me for a moment. "I don't know. I wish I did, believe me."

I let out a disappointed breath. I wasn't really surprised, just, it would've been nice if she knew. "Have you met any others?"

She shook her head, "No, you're the first. Have you?"

"Yes," I told her about Samuel.

"Wow. That's crazy."

A bus screeched to a stop. "I'm sorry, I gotta go," she said. "But hey, thanks for chasing after me. It's cool to know I'm not alone." She took the first seat and leaned her head against the window, closing her eyes. She was exhausted.

Me, Samuel, and now Adeline. For so many years I'd thought I was the only one.

Now I wondered how many of us there were out there. I tossed my soda can in the recycling bin and headed towards home.

And I remembered Nate and our impending 7:00pm appointment. Ugh.

TWENTY-THREE

I SAT WITH MY MOM on the sofa and stared at the walls. Mom had just finished painting them. "Looks good," I said.

"Thanks. There's something about a fresh coat of paint that just makes me, well, it sounds silly, but it makes me feel hopeful. The same way spring does, when the new leaves sprout."

"I don't think it's silly, Mom. I think it's cool."

We didn't talk much other than that. I didn't feel up to fluffy conversation, and I didn't think Mom did either. During one of the many cosmetic commercials we consumed in between news broadcasts, I made a decision. I was going to look good when Nate "non" broke up with me. He may feel this was something he had to do, but that didn't mean I had to make it easy for him. I headed upstairs.

My biggest task, as usual, was my hair. I added a fruity smelling hair product, combing it through with my fingers until every last rebellious strand had surrendered. It had a tint of sparkle in the shine, kind of like lip gloss, but for hair. It was down to my shoulder blades now, and I easily swept it up with a clip, letting a few loose ringlets frame my face. Next was a bit of make-up, not too much, just enough to look fresh and appealing, and then I changed into my favorite jean shorts and a cotton button down shirt, taking it easy with my arm. I slipped into a pair of flat leather sandals and viewed my image in the mirror. Not bad. Even my knees didn't seem that knobby anymore. In fact, everything was looking softer and rounder. In a good way. Eat your heart out, Nate.

The doorbell rang. I sprinted down the steps, wanting to beat my mother to the door, but too late. I could hear his voice, "Is Casey home?"

"Casey!" Mom shouted, practically in my ear.

"Ow, I'm right here, Mom."

"Oh sorry. Didn't hear you. Nate's here." She said this with her back half turned to Nate, giving me a questioning eyebrow. Mom invited him in.

"It's so nice to see you again, Nate."

"It's good to see you, too." He shoved his fists in his pockets and rocked on his shoes. It amused me. Meeting my mother made him nervous.

"There's a park a block away," I said, giving my mother the eye.

"You kids go on." She got the hint. "Have fun."

We started walking and I braced myself for his speech. Mental review: he didn't mean to hurt me, he just couldn't be my friend anymore. I pinched my eyes and waited.

"So tell me about it," Nate said.

"About what?" Maybe the speech was coming later. Of course, he needed to satisfy his curiosity first.

"About what it was like to go back to nineteen sixty-one."

Nate already possessed more of me than any other person I knew. I was so not about to give him any more. "It was okay. I told you everything at the hospital."

"Well, did anything happen?"

"What are you getting at?"

"No offense, but I've never seen you stay out of trouble, Casey."

I shrugged. He stopped and pulled me towards him. "Why don't you want to tell me?"

His hands firmly held my shoulders. Right on the sidewalk. In front of the neighbors and everything. The way he stared at me was so intense.

I couldn't breathe.

"You're hedging. What happened that you don't want to tell me?"

"Why should I tell you?" I swallowed hard. "Just say what you came to say, Nate. Let's get this over with."

He let his arms drop. "What are you talking about?"

Stupid me. My eyes prickled and I could tell my face was turning that unflattering shade of blotchy red. I stared at the sidewalk.

"Just tell me, you've had enough. Friendship with me is so much more than you bargained for, and you want to get on with your life. A normal life that doesn't include me. I understand. Just say it and go."

I felt his finger under my chin, sending electric shivers down my spine. He lifted my face, forcing me to look into his eyes.

"You got it all wrong," he whispered. "It drives me crazy that I might not be there next time you're in trouble. With all the Robert Willingsworths in the world, Casey, I want to be there with you, to protect you and to love you. Here and there."

Then he leaned down and kissed me. Kissed me! Hey, did he just say he loved me? My good arm reached up and grabbed his hair. He kissed me again, sweet, warm, soft kisses, and then touched my nose with his.

"Is this okay?"

"Yes!" He kissed me again. Every sensory in my body

screamed excitedly. Nate Mackenzie liked me, maybe even loved me.

When he pulled away, he said, "I'll be honest with you. I've agonized over this for weeks. It's why I kept distancing myself from you. It's true that life would be a whole lot simpler for me without you, Casey. But it would also be a whole lot emptier and quite a bit duller.

In the end I decided it didn't matter."

"But, I saw you with Jessica."

"What?"

"In the hall. It looked like you two were back together."

Nate shook his head. "I was just being gentlemanly." My cheeks tugged up in a grin as I remembered Sara Watson.

At the park, we settled on a bench and I snuggled close, completely happy. How differently this day had turned out.

"When did you realize that, well..." I didn't know how to say it. "That you liked me?"

Nate chuckled. "Ever since the first time we went back together and you showed me up with your expert hunting skills. You're a likable person."

I loved how his eyes sparkled when he smiled. "But, I realized it was more than that for me, that I was crazy over you when, well, when Willingsworth proposed. I was completely insane with jealousy. I tried to beat it down, but I couldn't win."

I laughed. "So, that's why you kept blowing hot and cold."

"Hey, go easy on me. It's not your usual love triangle."

He draped his arm around my shoulders. "So, back to the sixties?" he nudged. Though I really didn't want to, I told him about the run in with Jerome. Nate clenched his jaw and tightened his grip on my shoulder when I explained how I got away by stomping on Jerome's sneaker. I moved on to lighter things.

"Samuel has a pretty big family, three sisters and a brother." I told Nate their names and ages.

"Right, you'd mentioned Rosa."

"She was having a baby in the living room right when Samuel and I looped back to the Watsons'. I don't know what she had or if the baby was okay. I only know she wasn't going to keep it. They were too poor. All the kids had to work to support the family because their dad was murdered."

"That's harsh."

I agreed. "I really felt bad for her."

The sun had slid behind the horizon. "It's getting late," I said. "I have to get home."

Nate walked me back to my house and up the steps to the front door. Then he kissed me again. It wasn't a kiss good-bye. It was a see-you-tomorrow-and-everyday-after-that kind of kiss.

Nate was with me. Nate was mine. Nate Mackenzie and Casey Donovan. I liked the sound of that.

I couldn't wait to call Lucinda!

TWENTY-FOUR

MOTHERS' DAY.

"Mom, I told you I would make supper, so go relax."

The burritos were in the oven. I was shredding cheese for nachos. Mom opened the cutlery drawer and started digging. "I've already set the table," I reminded her. The weather was warm enough to eat outside, so I'd cleaned off the picnic table and put out our bright colored plastic picnic ware. I even picked some of the flowers in bloom and set them in a large jar in the middle of the table, going for a semi romantic look, because Dad was coming for dinner. Maybe something would spark between my parents.

I slid the nachos into the oven. Mom opened the fridge then closed it. She looked a little lost.

"Mom? Is everything okay?"

"Oh, yeah, I'm fine. I'll just take the drinks outside."

She went back to the fridge and removed the soda and juice, disappearing out the back door to the patio. I think Mom was nervous. Not in an I'm-filing-for-divorce-after-dessert nervous, but a this-is-kind-of-a-date nervous.

Yes! That explained the new spring dress she was wearing.

Dad arrived early. And he came with flowers.

"Hey, Dad." I greeted him with a squeeze.

"Hi, sugar. How are you?" He followed me into the kitchen.

"I'm good."

I opened the oven and took out the nachos. Whoa, almost burnt them.

"How's school?" His hands were still holding the bouquet of roses, his eyes darting around the kitchen looking for Mom.

"Fine and she's out back."

He nodded, took a breath and opened the back door. He looked kind of handsome today. And also nervous, like a school-boy. It was cute.

When everything was ready I called for Tim to help me take it out. Of course, he had his selective hearing on, and didn't come until everything was already done.

We were both stopped short to see Mom and Dad kissing. Yup, the this-is-a-date kind of kissing. Neither of us said anything. Then Mom told my dad thank you and accepted the roses.

"Here let me help," I said, setting the plates down. I picked up my garden flowers and dumped them out.

"Casey, I could've gotten another vase," Mom's face blushed as she dropped her bouquet into my offered empty jar. Dad asked Tim the obligatory questions, how he was and how was school, to which Tim grunted fine and fine.

Just before we were about to dig into a primo Mexican feast, there was a knock on the fence gate. Dad got up and opened it and an older African American gentleman, maybe in his late sixties, stepped stiffly into view. He removed his hat revealing a head of gray curly hair. He scanned our faces and zeroed in on mine.

His knees buckled and Dad grabbed his elbow. "Sir, are you all right?"

The man shook his head, all the while staring at me. He looked familiar. I broke out in goose bumps. My father persisted. "Is there something we can do for you?"

The man refocused on my dad. "So, sorry. Excuse my manners. I heard voices and took the liberty to come to your back yard." He extended his arm and shook my father's hand. "My name is Samuel Jones."

"S-Samuel?" I stood and sat down and then stood and sat again. "Do you know this man, Casey?" my mother said.

"Uh, yes, we met, uh, when my eighth grade class did community service at an old folks home?"

Samuel added quickly, "Yes, I was visiting my mother there."

"Come in, Mr. Jones," my father offered. "We were just about to eat. You can join us."

"Oh, I didn't mean to interrupt a family gathering."

"No!" I blurted. "I mean, yes, you must stay. Please come."

I quickly produced another garden chair and put it beside mine.

Samuel smiled and took it. I was giddy. Samuel was here! But why?

My mother passed the platter of burritos around and then the nachos and tossed salad. Samuel waited until she started eating before digging in. Tim seemed happy to have someone else take the spotlight, so he wouldn't have to talk.

"May I ask," my father began, "what brings you here?"

"Actually, you do."

I raised my eyebrows. Samuel's here for Dad? Not me?

"My sister gave up a baby for adoption when she was very young." He glanced at me, then back to my dad. "It's a complex story."

No. Way. Was he really going to say what I thought he was going to say? I rubbed the goose bumps on my arms.

"Ten years ago, she registered with the adoption agency in an effort to find her son."

My dad blanched a bit. Was he catching on? He said, "I'm adopted, but I think you know that. I just registered to find my birth parents after Christmas."

Ah, ha. So I'd gotten through to him when I encouraged him to do that.

"Yes, and that is why I'm here. To tell you that you found her."

"Rosa?" I whispered.

"Yes." He turned back to face my dad. "My sister Rosa is your mother. She is very ill and would like to see you before she passes from this earth. If you are willing?"

Oh. My. God! I knew there was a cosmic reason why I looped to 1961 with Samuel!

Tim held a nacho in the air, mid bite. This news was enough to stop even him from eating. My mother grabbed my father's hand. "Richard?"

"Yes, of course I'll see her."

"Great," Samuel said. "We can go tomorrow afternoon, if that works for you." Then he looked at me. "I think it would be best if Richard and your mother came alone."

I understood. Rosa wouldn't get why I hadn't aged in almost fifty years.

"She's too frail for large groups," he explained to everyone else. Dad asked Samuel a bunch of questions about Rosa and the whole Jones family. I loved hearing how all their lives had panned out. Samuel had never married, Rosa did but not until she was in her late thirties and had one child, a girl. That meant Dad had a half sister to meet. Jonah and the two girls had all gone on to be university graduates, making Mama proud. She'd passed on shortly after Yolanda had graduated from Harvard. He didn't get into the details of dad's birth, and why Rosa gave him up. Maybe he was saving that story for Rosa to tell.

Weird. I was almost a witness to my own father's birth. Hmm, not sure how I felt about that.

After the meal, I helped Mom clear the table while Dad asked Samuel more questions about his family. I had to find a way to get Samuel alone—I had my own questions. Tim had gone inside with Mom. I just had to find a way to get rid of Dad.

"Um, Dad?" I said, "Mom needs you in the kitchen."

She didn't really say that, but I thought it would be good for them to have a chance to talk alone, too, and by the way Dad jumped up to help her, I think he agreed.

Finally, I had Samuel to myself. "It's so great to see you again. Here. Wow."

"It's good to see you, too, Cassandra. You haven't changed a bit." His eyes crinkled as he laughed. "It must be strange for you to see me as such an old man."

"The life of a time traveler is nothing but strange," I said. "Do you still...?"

He shook his head. "Not for nearly fifteen years now. Nature must know I'm too old for that kind of life."

"It's so great to hear about Rosa and the others. So cool that we're family. Samuel, you're my uncle!"

He chuckled. "Strange but true."

"Uncle Sam," I said, laughing with him. His eyes widened like he'd just remembered something.

"I have something for you." He dug into his coat pocket and pulled out a tarnished silver cross necklace.

"My necklace! That's where I lost it?"

"Rosa found it in her bedroom. She wore it for years after you left. I think it reminded her of the baby she gave away. We both knew it was yours, but I never said anything."

He laid it carefully in my open hands. "I found it on her

dresser the last time I visited her. For some reason, I slipped it into my pocket..."

"Thanks for bringing it back to me, Samuel."

My parents brought out a tray with coffee and dessert, and we visited with Samuel until dusk. It was hard to say goodbye to Samuel when the cab arrived and he had to leave. I hugged him and promised I'd bring Nate and visit him sometime soon.

TWENTY-FIVE

FOR SOMEONE WHO DIDN'T DANCE, I sure was dancing a lot this year. This time it was the senior prom. Yes, THE Prom, and I was there (not Jessica, but I won't rub it in) with Nate.

My curls were shiny and tamed with a humongous amount of hair product. I had pinned the sides up, and the rest hung midway down my back. The newly polished silver cross hung around my neck. I wore a long lime green dress that my mother had helped me pick out (I'd promised her that she'd get to help me pick out my prom dress, even though technically it was Nate's prom, not mine), and regal looking white gloves that reached up to my elbows. I chose these for two reasons: one, to cover the angry red line on my forearm and two, to protect Nate. Even though he said he didn't mind going back, I didn't want to take any chances.

With one of his hands holding my gloved one and the other on the small of my back, he shuffled with me around the gym floor.

"You look absolutely beautiful, Casey," he said, smiling. For once, I actually believed him.

"And you are simply dashing," I said with a fake British accent. I was happier than happy.

Lucinda danced with Josh (a little match making on my part), and she gave me a sly thumbs up as they spun by. Tyson and Kelly nuzzled nose to nose.

"I'm really going to miss you, when you leave for Toronto, you know?" The thought of Nate leaving made me want to curl up in a fetal position. Why did I bring that up tonight, of all nights?

"Well, now that you mention it, I have a surprise for you."

"What?"

"I didn't want to say anything until I was absolutely sure."

"Nate!" His eyes sparkled. He enjoyed teasing me.

"I transferred to Boston University. I'm not leaving."

Eek! I let out a little squeal. "Really! You're not going? But what about your scholarship?"

"Still got that. I guess my skills are wanted."

Yay! "That's great news." I was so excited I couldn't help jumping up and down a little bit. In a graceful and ladylike fashion, of course.

The song ended, and an up tempo one started. Some couples left the floor, others just started dancing again. I waited for a cue from Nate, as to what he wanted to do. He didn't lead me off the floor. And he didn't start dancing. What he did made me gasp and shiver.

He peeled off my elbow length gloves.

"What are you doing?"

"You don't need these." He gently rubbed the scar on my arm with his thumb then held both of my hands in his, skin to skin. He lowered his head to kiss my face, tiny little butterfly kisses until he reached my mouth. Each kiss was a promise and a decla-ration. I could go back in time at any moment, and Nate would gladly go with me.

The End.

DON'T MISS the next book - ClockwiseR!

The last year has been smooth sailing for Casey Donovan. She and her boyfriend Nate are doing better than ever, and things at home are good, too. Everything's been so calm, she hasn't "tripped" back to the nineteenth century in ages.

Then the unthinkable happens and she accidentally

takes her rebellious brother Tim back in time. It's 1862 with the Civil War brewing, and for Tim this spells adventure and excitement. Finding himself stuck in the past, he enlists in the Union army, but it doesn't take long before he discovers real life war is no fun and games.

Casey and Nate race against the clock to find Tim, but the strain wears on their relationship. It doesn't help that the intriguing new boy next door has his sights on Casey, and isn't shy to let her know it.

Can Nate and Casey find Tim in time to save him? And is it too late to save their love?

Buy on Amazon or read for free on Kindle Unlimited!

Read on for an excerpt.

Check out the rest of The Clockwise Collection on Amazon!

FOR MORE INFORMATION about my books or how to follow me on social media, visit leestraussbooks.com

ABOUT THE AUTHOR

Lee Strauss is a USA TODAY bestselling author of The Ginger Gold Mysteries series, The Higgins & Hawke Mystery series (cozy historical mysteries), A Nursery Rhyme Mystery series (mystery suspense), The Perception series (young adult dystopian), The Light & Love series (sweet romance), The Clockwise Collection (YA time travel romance), and young adult historical fiction with over a million books read. She has titles published in German, Spanish and Korean, and a growing audio library.

When Lee's not writing or reading she likes to cycle, hike, and play pickleball. She loves to drink caffè lattes in exotic places, and eat dark chocolate anywhere.

www.leestraussbooks.com

If you enjoyed reading *Clockwise*, please help others enjoy it too.

Lend it: This ebook is lending-enabled, so please share with a friend.

Recommend it: Help others find the book by recommending it to friends, readers' groups, discussion boards and by suggesting it to your local library.

Review it: Please tell other readers why you liked this book by reviewing it at Amazon or Goodreads. If you do write a review, Let me know at **admin@leestraussbooks.com** so I can thank you.

Check out the rest of The Clockwise Collection on Amazon!

For more information about my books or how to follow Elle Lee Strauss on social media visit leestraussbooks.com

+ Follow on Amazon

CLOCKWISER

CASEY
Beginning of Summer Holidays

Sometimes I just wished I were an only child. But then, I guess I'd be walking or taking transit instead of getting a lift from Tim in his Cavalier beater. He didn't have air conditioning either, and the wind blowing in from our open windows was hot and moist. The humidity made me feel like I was wearing a warm wet wash-cloth for a shirt.

"Can't you drop me off first?" I said, fanning myself with my hand. I was meeting my best friend Lucinda at the mall where she worked at Forever21 and she only had a forty minute break. Plus, there was the added bonus of air conditioning there. Tim stubbornly refused, insisting that he had to stop at the ATM for some cash first.

"I'm not your personal taxi service, Casey," he snarled, turning the volume up on his stereo. The bass beat was so loud it rattled the trunk. "Get off your lazy butt and get your license already."

I gave him a dirty look and reached over to turn the music down. I had a very good reason for not getting my license, one I could never tell Tim or any member of my family. There were only three people, *currently living*, that knew the reason why. One of them was my boyfriend, Nate MacKenzie.

My heart still fluttered a bit when I thought of him in those terms. *My boyfriend.* Not just some out of reach guy I crushed hard on my whole sophomore year who was totally out of my league, but my *boyfriend.*

We'd already been an official couple for an entire year, totally blowing all the doomsday predictions that we'd never make it. No one thought a college boy would stick it out with a junior in high school (especially Nate's former evil girlfriend!)

But he did, and we were still going strong. I'd be entering my senior year in a few weeks and then I'd go to Boston University, too.

"If you dropped me off first, you wouldn't have to deal with me." I tried to reason.

"If I didn't shuttle you around at all I wouldn't have to deal with you."

The only reason he did was because my parents were putting the screws in. Tim's bad attitude, questionable choice of friends and poor grades put him in their bad books. Driving me around was penance.

Tim pulled into the parking lot of the bank and hopped out, leaving the car running. I reached over and turned it off. Idling the car was bad for the environment for one, and a waste of Tim's hard earned minimum wage job money. You'd think he'd know better.

I checked the time on my phone and grew anxious as Lucinda's break time grew nearer. Tim had his back to me as he stood in line at the ATM window. I checked my reflection in the visor mirror. Since I'd grown out of my skinny awkwardness last year, (and of course, snagged a hot boyfriend) I was more mindful of my looks. Instead of trying to hide behind a bush of dark curly hair, I took care of it with hair products and good salon cuts. I was happy with the way my curls framed my face now. I took a tube of lip gloss out of my purse and rolled it onto my lips.

I tugged on my shorts and rubbed my bare legs. They were so long, my knees almost touched the glove compartment. Height had its advantages, but getting comfortable in a small car wasn't one of them.

I turned the radio on and hummed along with the top forty. I daydreamed about me and Nate and how we could relax for the rest of the summer, hopefully stretching the lazy days out as long as possible.

I checked the time on my phone and immediately started stressing about being late to meet Lucinda. C'mon, Tim! He was second in line now. I texted Lucinda to let her know I might be a little late.

I heard sirens in the area and I perked up. This wasn't the best neighborhood. The bank wasn't huge, just tucked into a strip mall along with a nail place, a dollar store, and a thrift shop. Litter overflowed from the bin and a good amount had been blown up against the cement foundation.

I checked on Tim. He'd finally made it to the front, the last one in line. If I'd known it was going to take him this long, I would've ran into the dollar store and picked up cheap nail polish.

The siren noise grew increasingly louder and suddenly three cop cars pulled into the parking lot beside me. My heart jumped and I thought fleetingly that maybe Tim was in trouble with the law again, except that he was getting money out of the ATM, not robbing the bank.

But someone was.

Everything happened so fast.

A guy with a ski mask pushed past Tim as he ran out the bank doors. A cop shouted, "stop or I'll shoot." Another masked man followed. Guns went off.

I heard myself shout, "Tim!" He was right in the middle of the cross fire!

He stood there, stunned and frozen. A police officer ran to him, pushing him to the ground, just as the second armed man shot in their direction. The officer fell to the ground taking the bullet instead of Tim.

The robbers ran around the corner and out of sight, chased by police officers on foot and a cruiser down the back alley.

I sprinted to Tim where he was on the ground by the fallen cop.

"Are you okay?"

His face was white and he motioned to the woman beside him. "Yeah, but I don't think she is."

The officer moaned, holding her hand on her chest.

"Oh, ma'am, are you okay?" I searched for blood but couldn't see any.

"I will be," she said gasping for breath. "I have a vest on."

Another officer kneeled beside her. "Ambulance is on its way."

The woman had dark hair pulled back in a low bun. Her eyes stayed pinched together and her pale face glistened with sweat. The impact of the bullet was enough to do some damage. I picked up her police hat that had fallen off her head and handed it to her.

"Thank you," I said.

"Just doing my duty."

The ambulance arrived. The paramedics pushed us aside and lifted the woman onto a gurney.

The cop who'd checked her pulse stepped forward from his opened door cruiser. Radio dispatch noises leaked out.

I watched the ambulance pull away, siren blasting, and realized I didn't know her name. I asked the officer standing beside me.

"That's Officer Clarice Porter," he said. "Now, would you two mind coming with me to the station to file a report?"

We agreed and I took my first ride in a police car. It was Tim's second, the first was not for noble reasons. He still claimed it was his friend Alex and not him that had stolen the cigarettes from the convenience store.

A thought like a loud banner ran through my mind as the doors of the police cruiser slammed shut and we drove away.

Clarice Porter saved my brother's life.

Buy on Amazon or read for free on Kindle Unlimited!

ACKNOWLEDGEMENTS

The biggest shout out has to go to my lovely daughter, Tasia Strauss. Not only was she my muse for this book, she gave me great plot ideas, her editorial chops, plus her faith in me as a writer has been unwavering. My husband Norm is a close second, always affirming and supporting me on this long, exciting and sometime tumultuous journey. Also, my three sons and my parents, for being such an important part of my life.

Thank you to my former agents, Natalie Fischer and Taylor Martindale, for believing in CLOCKWISE and for excellent editorial advice.

Thanks also to Denise Jaden and Juanita Wenham who have been there for the long run.

My on-line friends in the trenches, Sara Larson, Anne Riley, Talli Rolland, Tamara Hart Heiner, Leigh Moore, Laurel Garver, Heather McCorkle, Laura Pauling, Caroline Starr Rose and Elena Johnson for willingly and eagerly being a pivotal part of my blog tour, and more importantly for all the extra behind the scenes support. It's been so great getting to know you, and hope-fully someday we can meet in person. There are many, many more wonderful people I've met on-line, and I can't be more thankful to be part of such an amazing writing community.

Thanks also to all my Wattpad fans for loving Clockwise. I so appreciated your support and encouraging words.

My Noble Girls, Donna Petch, Shawn Giesbrecht and Norine Stewart, for all your love, prayers and support—so grateful to have you in my life.

Thank YOU, the reader! I hope you liked CLOCKWISE, and if you're reading the acknowledgements, then you deserve a double thanks and chocolate chip cookies!

And most of all, to Jesus, who gives my life meaning.

Lightning Source UK Ltd.
Milton Keynes UK
UKHW010634100822
407113UK00001B/378